PEBBLES

SHORT STORIES

CHIP TOLSON

Pebbles
Short Stories

Spiderwize
Remus House
Coltsfoot Drive
Woodston
Peterborough
PE2 9BF

www.spiderwize.com

A CIP catalogue record for this book is available from the British Library.

ISBN: 978-1-911113-68-3

Pebbles lie on the seashore in their multitudes waiting to be found. Sometimes one or two are picked up, maybe even kept and taken home to be looked at from time to time. More often, after a cursory glance, they are cast out to sea, perhaps bouncing and making a splash before they disappear.

In the hope that some of the stories in this volume, some shorter, some longer, will be noticed, they lie waiting on these pages. I hope they give enjoyment before the waves reclaim them.

FOREWORD

These stories have been written in recent years and reflect the everyday in people's lives, younger people and older people. They reflect peacetime and times of war over many decades. A few of these tales have won prizes.

Some are set in my home territory of Exmoor and the West Country, others in the Western Isles of Scotland, islands I have visited and sailed around on many occasions, and some in other parts. In general, the stories stem from the places I have been and the people I have met, not that anyone will recognise themselves within these pages.

There are many individuals who have given me support and encouragement over the years since I redirected my energies into writing fiction after an interesting and enjoyable career in the international ship-owning industry.

I thank all those involved with the Yeovil Writing Group who have listened, critiqued and encouraged work in progress. I have benefitted from their opinions.

Above all, there has been the constant support and encouragement of my wife and I dedicate this volume of stories to Clare, with my love.

Chip Tolson,

Withiel Florey, Somerset, UK

www.chiptolson.com

CONTENTS

BOOKS FOR ALICE

A dark midwinter morning with rain blowing in through the open garage doors, straight off a wind-whipped Bristol Channel; ten minutes for checking the bookshelves then he would be away on his moorland round.

The phone rang in the garage office; he ignored it, getting on with his stock check.

'It was for you, Fred,' she called out, holding open the office window.

'The name is Frederick.'

'You're not to take the library out,' she shouted back, adding 'Fred', to be annoying.

'Who says?'

'The Town Office.'

'If I want to go out, I will.'

'They said to tell you.' She banged the window closed.

Frederick strode over to the wooden office shed in the corner of the council garage; a warm blast of room freshener greeted him. 'What's it got to do with them?'

'They said it's going to snow; they're ordering the gritters out.'

'Well, ring them back. I've already left.'

Squeaking wiper blades flipped a rhythm across the windscreen. The library van climbed the winding ascent to Wheddon Cross past lofty beech trees reaching up to their leafless canopy and a blackening sky, rivulets from the past night's rain tumbled down gullies draining to the valley.

Frederick let the library van grind its slow progress up to the village and his first stop of the day in the car park outside 'The Rest and Be Thankful Inn'. Next, he would drive ten miles on moorland roads, stopping at farms and cottages until his lunchtime call on Alice. Whatever weather was threatened, Frederick had to get to Alice, infirm and bed-bound in her lifetime cottage home.

Snowflakes fluttered onto the windscreen.

The front door was off the latch. 'How are you today?'

'I can't complain.'

'You never do, Alice.' Her small shape wrapped in a woollen shawl by the morning nurse was propped on pillows stacked up against a brass bedstead in her unchanging front room.

'Put the kettle on, Frederick.'

'I've got a good collection for you today, Alice. Two new biographies, several romances and a P.D. James you haven't read.'

Her impish grin smiled her reply. She waved a frail hand towards the books piled on the dresser.

'These all finished, Alice? I'm giving you extra for the holidays as I won't be back until late January.'

'I didn't expect to see you today. Look at that weather forecast.' She nodded at the television playing a summary: *Blizzards on Exmoor, drifting in high winds.*

It was always the same routine; he made a pot of tea and heated a tin of soup. Cream of tomato he'd brought today, her favourite. His three-weekly lunchtime breaks with Alice boosted his spirits for the rest of the day.

The Town Office had got it right. The van left tracks along winter roads waiting for the gritting lorries. Frederick glanced at his mobile clipped to the dashboard; he should have had it turned on. He bent forward to squint through the arc the wipers were clearing, keen to get to his afternoon stops. Surprised borrowers, summoned with a toot on his horn from farmhouse kitchen warmth, trod slush into his van.

Snow was settling when he reached his last call outside the Village Hall at Kings Execombe.

The van climbed away from the village following in wheel lines pressed out by a tractor up the hill; footprints ran alongside the tracks, sometimes stepping in the wheel marks, sometimes in the snow.

The bend on the hill loomed. A distance further and the road flattened out across the plateau to join the main road. The bend came. Frederick sat rigid in his seat, willing the van up the hill, creeping along the guiding wheel marks made by the tractor. A figure loomed up hardly visible in the swirling snow, a person standing back carrying shopping bags. Stop now and be lost, the van churned on up the hill only coming to a stop in the middle of the road once it reached the level.

The doors opened with a hydraulic hiss. Snow swirled in, settling on the bookshelves and over his sweater. Looking back in the mirror he could just make out a figure trying to run in the library van's tracks.

'Have you got far to go?' he called. 'Oh, it's you, Mrs H.'

'Frederick, bless you. I thought you weren't going to stop.'

'I couldn't stop on the hill. Come into the van, you must be frozen.'

'My feet are like ice and the wet is through my coat.'

'You weren't in the village.'

'The late bus isn't running, I thought I better not wait. It isn't easy walking, mind.'

'Mrs H, it's two miles to your farm. I'll give you a lift.'

'It's off your route, Frederick. Drop me at the lane, that'll do me.'

'I can get you closer than that.'

The hissing doors closed, captive snow melting in the van's heat. Mrs H, her glasses steamed up, shook the wet snow from her hair and sat heavily in the passenger seat. Frederick wiggled the reluctant gear lever, crunched into gear and pulled away through deepening snow. At the fork in the road they branched away from the tractor's track into a narrow lane with high beech hedges keeping the snow at bay.

'This isn't too bad, Mrs H. I'll get you home.'

'Watch out at the bend, Frederick. Snow always drifts through the wire fence where the hedge-bank stops.'

'We'll be OK.'

But they weren't.

Deep snow lay across the lane. Frederick lost his bearings. White beneath, white above, a blur in-between and a genie gave the van a life of its own. It bumped and bucked, broke the fence down and set off downhill on a toboggan run into the valley ploughing over the steep snow-covered field.

'Hang on, Mrs H,' Frederick yelled, the steering wheel wrenched from his grasp, the van sliding into white oblivion, nothing but swirling snow.

They hit something solid, the van tipped at an angle, the engine stalled and a cascade of books tumbled from the shelves.

'Oh, my word, I've done it now. Are you hurt, Mrs H?'

She shook her head. They sat in silence staring at each other, waiting for whatever would be next.

'Will they find us, Frederick?' she whispered when all had been still for a while.

'I've tried my mobile; I can't get any signal. The van is painted yellow they'll see us well enough when the blizzard stops.'

'I could walk home.'

'I don't think so.' Frederick pointed at the window in the side door revealing a solid white wall. 'We're in a drift.' The van shuddered again, settling further over to its side, more books tipping from the shelves onto his legs. 'We're here for the night, Mrs H. There's a torch somewhere.'

'I've got biscuits in my shopping, and a cake.'

'And I've got a full flask of coffee.'

'We'll get by, Frederick. I'm sorry I took you out of your way.'

Frederick sat on the pile of library books, looking at the empty shelves tilting above him. Pale grey light filtered through the roof lights.

'Will you be in trouble, Frederick?'

'I guess I will, Mrs H. There was a message telling me not to go out today, but I couldn't let Alice down. She needs her books over Christmas. Do you want coffee, Mrs H?'

'Coffee and a slice of cake with a choice of books to read; what could be better?'

'You'll have read most of my books, Mrs H.'

'Not a single one.'

'What do you mean? You're a regular.'

'And I never read any of them. Mother reads them all; I don't have time for reading.'

'None of them?'

'I read half of one last summer. Mother insisted it go back as she'd finished it.'

'Perhaps I can find it for you.'

'Catherine Cookson, I remember that, about the Great War with a picture of a young woman and a man in uniform on the cover.'

'Cookson. It'll be in this pile somewhere. That's her shelf, marked "C", with the whole lot on the floor.'

The torch gave poor light for Frederick to read aloud. Mrs H had joined him on the pile of books, sharing the rug he kept in the van, their backs against the shelves. The coffee was finished and two slices of cake cut with his penknife had been eaten.

'Will they find us soon?'

'I hope so Mrs H, it'll be cold by morning.'

'You're a good lad, Frederick,' she yawned. 'Books for Alice, whatever the weather, and now you're reading me to sleep. Did she write many books?'

'Catherine Cookson? Yes, dozens, and she sold millions. All of them romances.'

'Did she ever write one about a middle-aged farmer's wife spending the night in the library van with a handsome young librarian?'

EVERYONE IS TALKING ABOUT IT

She'd been told there would be a three-month probationary period, a long way to go, it being only the third Monday meeting Amanda Chater had chaired. Monday reviews were a routine as old as the department store itself. Sharp at 10 o'clock on the first morning of every working week the heads of section gathered in the boardroom to run through a standing agenda of topics. They had gone easy on Amanda for the past two weeks; she knew it wouldn't last. You don't get promoted over the heads of long-serving staff members and not pick up resentment along the way.

'The bootleg trousers, the ones made in China, we've had many complaints about the seam stitching.' Mrs Prichard was speaking. Amanda had started work at the department store five years before as a junior in Maggie Prichard's section. Maggie had been twenty years at Meadows working her way up to be a section head.

Meadows hadn't been Amanda's first choice of career; she'd planned to be a lawyer. You need a law degree for that and she'd missed out on her chance of getting into university. Still she had got her Business Studies Diploma at college, moved a hundred miles from home to find employment and Meadows were good employers. Now she was making her mark in the company.

Amanda knew there had been gossip, a nod and a wink between the section heads, implying her promotion was prompted by the General

Manager's roving eye. That was unfair. She got on well with 'Mr Frank', he was certainly good-looking and a bachelor, but it was hard work that had won her the promotion and she was determined to show she was chosen on merit.

'Has the problem been taken up with the buyers?'

'We should never have gone to unknown Far East manufacturers. We should have stayed with the British factories we know.' Mrs Prichard looked at the nodding heads around the table. 'They wouldn't allow poor seam stitching out of the factory.'

'But at a price; we have to compete. It's the economics of the marketplace.'

'It's shoddy cost-cutting, if you ask me.' Mrs Prichard was determined to have her say and Amanda knew it was true. The Chinese orders had been hastily put in place to catch a fashion surge.

'It's economics and a matter of quality control,' she insisted looking Maggie in the eye, yet sensing the meeting was against her. 'There is no reason why these Far East goods should be below standard. We have to ensure proper quality control at the factories.'

Without any warning the boardroom door burst open. Charlie Potts looked around the room. There was something amiss, he was not his usual smart security presence.

'Sorry, is Mr Frank in?' Sgt Potts, for many years a soldier, now the morning shift Security Supervisor, was flustered.

'He's away, Charlie. He won't be back until tomorrow,' Amanda told him. Was she imagining the glimmer of resentment on Mrs Prichard's face? No one had told Maggie that Frank Meadows, the third generation to own and manage Meadows Department Store, had gone away. 'Is there a problem on the floor, Charlie?'

'Big time, Miss Chater.'

'What is it?'

'We've pulled shoplifter, a posh lady; she's kicking up a fuss; says she's Lady something and a friend of the Chief Constable.'

'And was she shoplifting?'

'Yes, got her positive on the CCTV, more than once, woollens and costume jewellery.'

'Well?'

'There's nothing on her, clean as a whistle, she must have dumped it.'

'Can you give her a warning?'

'Says she's going to sue us; can you come and have a word with her, Miss Chater.'

One by one the faces around the table turned to Amanda. It wouldn't wait. 'Yes, I'll come. Mrs Prichard, will you take over the meeting. I may be a while.'

Maggie Prichard took heart from her preferment over the other heads of section. 'I will, Miss Chater.'

In her office Amanda checked herself in the mirror, pursing her lips, confident she had been right to colour her hair auburn and pleased she had chosen her dark pinstripe suit to start the week. She decided to put on her gold frame Gucci glasses to look older

Sgt Potts worked the controls of Amanda's monitor in the corner of the room, bringing up two sections from the security tape. The woman was seen in both tapes, confident and skilled. In a flash a sweater and scarf disappeared inside her coat.

'She's done that before,' Amanda ran the tape back and watched the woman again.

'She's a professional if you ask me,' agreed Charlie. 'That's why she ditched the stuff before we got to her.'

'And nothing has been found in any of the usual places?'

'Nothing, but they're still searching.'

'Let's go.' Amanda didn't enjoy confrontation, but it went with the territory. Frank Meadows would use his charm in this situation; she had to do it her way. She gave a thin smile to Sgt Potts as they got out of the lift on the ground floor and made their way through to the back office.

The interview room was stark, a plain table with four upright chairs, a microphone and tape recorder. There had been a bottle of water and glasses until a recent accused had grabbed the bottle and struck out at Sgt Potts.

The woman was seated, heavily made up and, Amanda guessed, wearing a wig. Her coat had once been expensive, but might have been found in any charity shop. Ignoring the woman's disdain Amanda introduced herself as the Deputy General Manager of the store.

'And do you know who I am?'

'Sgt Potts has told me you are Lady Butler-Perkins, Madam.'

'And my husband is a respected member of the House of Lords.'

'That may be, Madam. We have reason to believe you took goods in this store, intending not to pay for them.'

'Don't be ridiculous, how dare you make such accusations.'

'You were recorded on camera, Madam. A sweater, a scarf and some costume jewellery.' There was no way this woman was going to let slip any hint of her guilt. Without the goods being found on her, even with the CCTV tape evidence, there was little chance of obtaining a conviction. Amanda needed to find a way of ending the interview in the store's favour.

A knock on the door and a folded note was handed to Sgt Potts; he looked at it briefly before passing it to Amanda. The single word "nothing" was written on the paper.

'I'm going to sue your tin-pot store for punitive damages. You see if I don't. I'll bankrupt you.'

There was a familiarity about this woman, not of her dress or her style, but something about her face. Had Amanda seen her in the store on another day, perhaps her picture in the local paper opening a fete with her lordly husband at her side? They were going to have to let her go. Amanda was not concerned at the woman's boast of friendship with the Chief Constable, an old chestnut. She feared there would be mutterings on the shop floor that the incident had been poorly handled; it wasn't the crisis she wanted Frank Meadows to come back to, not after the Directors had put their trust in her to run the business in the General Manager's absence.

The woman took out a packet of cigarettes, fiddling with her lighter, flipping it over in her hand.

Amanda remembered.

'This is no smoking area, Madam.'

'Your Ladyship, if you don't mind,' came the belligerent rejoinder.

'Oh, come on, cut the crap. You are no more a lady than I am.'

The woman sat open-mouthed a cigarette halfway to her lips. Sgt Potts stared at Amanda. For a moment the small room was hushed, just the hum of the tape recorder. Amanda's stomach churned.

'How dare you, impudent woman. I'll see that you lose your job for this.'

'Beacon Street Comprehensive, Snaresborough, 1993.' The shot struck home; the woman couldn't speak for a moment; Sgt Potts eased into his chair. Amanda stared across the table as the woman hesitated to meet her eye.

'I have no idea what you mean.'

'I think you do. The sixth form, set B.'

'You're talking gibberish, woman. I wish to leave and you will be hearing from my solicitor.'

'You will not be leaving until you have signed an undertaking never to visit this store again. And we will be reporting this matter to the police.'

'This is outrageous. I wish to leave.' The woman pushed back her chair. Sgt Potts strode across to the door to bar the woman's way.

'I wish to telephone my husband, Lord Butler-Perkins. Get me a telephone,' the woman was shouting.

'Do you recall the matter of the crib sheet found under a desk after the mathematics exam?'

The woman's face reddened, beads of sweat broke out on her upper lip. 'Who are you?'

'I told you when we first met. I am the Deputy General Manager of this department store. It was not just that one senior schoolgirl had been cheating in the exam; what mattered was that the cheat put the blame onto a younger girl in her set.'

'This has nothing to do with me. I demand that you let me pass. I am leaving.'

'Mary Richards, you don't know when to stop digging do you. I know who you are, I know what you did, and the girl you framed is well known to me. You are not Lady anyone, you are a habitual shoplifter and I expect, if we review past CCTV tapes, we will see that you have been shoplifting in this store on previous occasions.'

A broad smile crossed Sgt Potts' face as a strained intake of breath preceded the woman's tears. 'I'm desperate. It's true I'm not Lady anybody, and my pathetic husband has deserted me.'

'Sgt Potts, you can deal with the formalities. Please ensure that Ms Richards signs the usual undertaking and that all store detectives are given her description. I have business to attend to upstairs.' Amanda stood up and turned to the woman, 'Mary, let this be a warning to you. What you have done today is wrong, whatever your motivation; what you did at the time of those examinations was despicable. The young schoolgirl you framed lost her opportunity to take her exams that summer and didn't get to university.'

'It's just my rotten luck to come all this way from Snaresborough to get sussed by a hometown girl. Look in the Lloyd Loom laundry baskets if you want to find your wretched goods,' she said with a resigned air. Amanda threw a questioning glance at Charlie Potts. Surely someone had looked in the laundry baskets?

Amanda sat behind her desk with her eyes closed, willing the turmoil she felt inside to settle. Many times she had tried to forget that summer of disappointment. Now for the first time she felt she had exorcised the ghost.

There was a knock at her door; it was Maggie Prichard.

'Amanda, I've been on to the buyers and given them a roasting on the China products. They admit they didn't put proper quality control in place. Oh, and well done with the shoplifter. Everyone is talking about it.'

FRENCH CRICKET

Arguing got him nowhere. Storming from the headmaster's study, Peter fled the school buildings, desperate no one should see his disappointment, the swing doors crashing back behind him. He wrenched his bicycle from the rack, kicked down on the pedals and swept out into the main road without regard for oncoming traffic, head down he raced home through the rain.

His mother called from the kitchen after the front door slammed, the only answer was the thump of pounding feet on stair treads taking her son up the dogleg stairs to his room before resonating electronic rhythms throbbed down from the top of the house.

Peter sprawled on his bed, panting from the mad dash home. He'd show them, he'd smash the ball to kingdom come in Saturday's game. He should have been given the cricket ground work experience.

Fish pie, crusted with mashed potato browned under the grill, buttered peas, tomato ketchup and a shared can of lager. His mother knew the way to Peter's heart.

He broke his silence complaining that the miserable git Billy Walters was going to the County Ground for a week's work experience. In answer to her question, he told her he was going to an organisation called Old Concern.

'They help the elderly. It could be rewarding, Peter.'

'I'm much better at cricket than Billy.'

‘Perhaps that’s the point. You’ll get to see another side of life. Mrs Carter runs Old Concern, it’s a good organisation.’

His mother was right; Mrs Carter was efficient, the Old Concern office worked long hours, staffed by volunteers, but mounds of paper built up beside the seldom used computer. Peter set about building a database to the relief of the volunteers who’d shirked the task. Soon the desks in the office were clear of the piles of paper.

‘This afternoon you must come out with me on a visit, Peter. I’m going to see Sandy; one of our special pensioners.’ Enid Carter smiled at the reluctant look on the boy’s face.

Mrs Carter knocked on Sandy’s front door; she didn’t wait for an answer going in to the cramped flat. An old man was dozing, his cardigan rucked up behind him in his armchair, his mouth hanging open, breath rasping from watery lungs. A fuzzy-pictured television flickered light into the room, a dewdrop hung from the old man’s nose. Disinfectant pervaded the air.

Eyes blinking, the pensioner woke looking at the incomers through misty eyes.

‘Hello, Sandy. I was passing and thought we would drop in to see you; I’ve brought a young man with me, this is Peter.’ The small figure looked across at his unknown visitor with a quizzical stare.

‘Hello, Sir,’ ventured Peter with the formality of the schoolroom, trying not to look at the drip on the old man’s nose.

‘Let’s have tea, Sandy.’ Without pausing for a reply she pointed Peter through a door off the living room to get the kettle boiling.

The kitchen was cluttered, unwashed plates and saucepans with loose handles were piled up; gas spluttered as he put the heavy kettle onto the flame.

Over tea, with the cakes they'd bought on the way over, Mrs Carter told Sandy Ingles about Peter captaining Bishop Melchett School's First Eleven, soon off to Paris to play in a Schools' International Cricket Tournament. Sandy, now fully awake from his nap, looked up at the tall lad from the hollow of his chair.

'You'll be a bowler, do you seam or spin, lad?' His voice was strained, cake crumbs tumbling down his cardigan.

Peter brightened at the old man's interest, he claimed to bowl a bit of spin, off breaks, but saying he was mainly a batsman coming in at number three. Peter saw a glint in Sandy's eye. The old man pointed to a photograph propped on a shelf amongst old books, a photo of a group of flannelled men in blazers staring toward the camera, the picture had faded with the light of passing decades. The legend read "County versus Australia - 1948". Peter looked at it in growing wonderment.

'Are you Alexander Ingles, *the* Sandy Ingles, who got a hat-trick against the Australians in 1948?'

The old man beamed.

'Including Bradman?'

'It was a grand day.' The crouched figure deep in his chair chuckled.

Peter took the tea mugs and plates through to the kitchen. The water came hot after he let it run. The pile of dirty crocks on the draining board was soon washed as he tried to remember the names of the County players in the nineteen-forties and fifties, the names listed on wooden boards at the back of the Members' Stand. In the distance, through the murky window, he saw the clock overlooking the County Ground. It was raining. He smiled, thinking Billy Walters might be getting wet.

As they walked back to the office, Mrs Carter suggested there should be a security lock fitted on Sandy's front door.

Peter volunteered.

Most afternoons after school, Peter cycled to Sandy's flat with his spare key for the front door to talk about cricket, wash the dishes, clean the sink and take rubbish out to the wheelie bin in the forecourt. Most days he checked the fridge to see if there were things he could get from the supermarket.

Old scrapbooks were piled in a corner on the threadbare carpet, bulging with yellowed newspaper cuttings, match reports of County games in the fifties, the sixties and a few in the seventies remembered with pride. Peter read them aloud as Sandy chipped in with memories and gossip about teammates.

'Did you play cricket at school in Scotland?'

Sandy told him of his boyhood in his coal mining community, the village team keen as mustard in the Ayrshire League. His headmaster was captain; he might have played all his cricket there if the war hadn't come and taken him into the army, playing for his regiment, scratch games wearing khaki and hobnail boots; it was there he turned to spin bowling. Something he could do to good advantage and he never went back to the pit, never went back to Ayrshire.

Months spent on Aldershot Heath, freezing in February, burning in May then across to France, seasick all the way over, to wade ashore onto the Normandy beaches three days into the invasion. In no time they were on the front line. Sandy was lucky, many weren't, they were young lads, not much older than Peter.

'Did you get any medals?'

'A few, they're in a drawer by the bed, nothing grand, just the handouts,' the old man chuckled at the lad, always on the go, looking at everything. The flat was tidy now, tidier than it had been for a long time. He had to thank the lad for that. Seventeen was a lifetime ago, half five sharp each morning at the pithead as an electrician's apprentice; a few years learning his trade then the war.

Peter found Sandy's tattered medal ribbons with his army pay-book: INGLES, Alexander, with "Private" crossed out and overwritten "Lance Corporal". He found a scuffed cricket ball, dark with age, in the same drawer.

A smile creased Sandy's face as he took the ball in his hand. His shaking fingers with swollen knuckles looking for their grip. His wrist arched over, his fingers circling the ball to hold the seam.

'That was the one that did him, that was how I got him. Bradman didn't pick it.' He handed the ball back for Peter to keep, there being little point hiding it away in a pensioner's drawer. He urged the lad to have a ball in his hand whenever he could, to get his fingers on it, twist his wrist and play with the ball.

Peter took the ancient ball from Sandy's gnarled hand smelling the leather worn with age and sensed the essence of summer wickets and cheering crowds.

Sandy had seldom spoken of his months in France, not even to Jane, his wife for twenty-seven contented years. Every summer spending weeks away travelling to far-off fixtures. It was almost twenty-five years since Jane had died alone in a hospital bed as he sat anxious on a rattling southbound train released a day early from the game in Scarborough.

His French war memories flooded back as Peter leafed through his scrapbooks. He heard again the gunfire attacking their positions, sensing the stench of cordite; they'd fired, the enemy had fired and young men were left dying on the battlefield. He hoped Peter would never see the like of it in his lifetime.

Sandy was at ease talking with the lad of his soldiering, of the clammy fear in his stomach on the Normandy beaches, the smell of death, the scent of summer flowers and woodlands as his battalion fought their way across the countryside reaching Paris "en fete" as the shackles of war were thrown off. As a true Scottish soldier Sandy had marched along the Champs-Élysées in his kilt.

'The lassies loved it. My, it was a bonny time.'

The young soldiers had known life would never be the same. They were quartered near Paris through the spring, the war was ending, blossom was on the trees and they would soon be home.

He'd never been back, not to the cemeteries, maybe he would have enjoyed seeing Paris again, maybe not. Peter looked up from the scrapbook he'd been reading.

'Our tournament is in Paris.'

'We went there as liberators. You mark my words lad; you'll come of age in Paris. I wish I were young again.'

'But we're going for the tournament, for the cricket.'

'Play your cricket, take your wickets, score your runs and when you're done on the cricket field, go into the Paris night.'

Packing his bags for the Easter tournament, Peter told his mother what he knew about the famous cricketer, Alexander Ingles, the man who got a hat-trick against Australia, or all he wanted his mother to know about the old man and his war time weeks in France. He worked the seam of a ball with his fingers, showing his mother the many finger grips Sandy had taught him.

The tournament was a success for Bishop Melchett's. They might have reached the final if their "semi" against an Australian team hadn't been rained off to give a "Duckworth Lewis" win to their opponents, batting second. Peter did well, a forty and an unbeaten sixty off his bat in the early rounds, but best of all he was the only player to take five wickets in an innings, thinking of Sandy with every ball, adjusting his grip, imagining the great Australian facing him at the batting crease. And he had another tale to tell Alexander Ingles when he got back from Paris, something off the cricket field.

When he opened the local paper back home after his fortnight in the tournament, there were two reports to read. One spoke of the school's successes in the tournament, the other headed the obituaries. A tribute by the Chairman of the County Cricket Club told of Ingles' career for the county and of his great bowling feat against the Australians.

Peter sat towards the back at the crematorium. As the congregation filed out, a hand gripped his shoulder. He turned, recognising the captain of the County Cricket team.

'It's Peter isn't it, the lad from the Paris tournament. Sandy spoke about you when I saw him in the hospital.'

'I never had the chance to tell him how it went.'

'Don't worry lad, he knew all about it. Come down to the nets tomorrow morning, I want to see you bowl.'

THERE WERE A LOT OF STRAY DOGS IN GROZNY

'How about over there?' Svetlana, pointing at a place far back amongst the pavement tables, combed stained fingers through her cropped dark hair and took out a pack of cigarettes.

'You promised to give up smoking,' Kate challenged her protégée.

'I will, I need this.' She lit up, inhaled and waved at a waitress.

Something had happened, she had spoken only pleasantries since Kate greeted her at Funchal airport off the second London flight she'd met that morning; Svetlana had never been good over timings.

'I'm sorry you've had your hair cut short.'

'It'll grow again. It wasn't wise to be too feminine out there. I need a drink.'

'Was it bad?'

'Yes.' Bitten fingernails gave scant purchase on the label she was teasing from the packet. 'It was bad.' Svetlana exhaled and watched the plume of spent smoke curl toward the canvas awning.

A waitress edged over between chairs pushed back by overweight tourists.

'Wine?'

'Dry white for me.'

‘Let’s have champagne.’

‘Whatever for?’

‘To celebrate my being here.’

‘If it’s what you want.’

‘After the squalor of past weeks, it’s what I must have.’

The waitress put menus on the table and went to get their wine.

‘I feel better already.’ Svetlana, stubbing out her half-smoked cigarette, smiled, masking a glimpse of tears behind her evasive eyes.

‘Do you want to talk?’

‘No, not here… not yet,’ she looked around at neighbouring tables laden with wine, with beer and food piled high on plates.

‘What are they having?’ she pointed at skewers of diced meat on a nearby table.

‘Espetada; beef and peppers, cooked with herbs.’

‘It looks good.’

‘I ate here yesterday; it is good. I’ll settle for an omelette tonight.’

The waitress returned with champagne, pulling an ice bucket stand from the service station. The wine bubbled, Svetlana chose the diced beef and took a mouthful of champagne. ‘It tingles,’ she blinked and sniffed.

‘You will tell me what happened?’

‘Later.’

This was not the bright-eyed undergraduate Kate remembered appearing in the newsroom one wet day on her long vacation, asking if they could use a bilingual English/Russian speaker on their staff. They couldn’t, yet there was an excitement about the young woman. Kate told her she could tag along for a few days without pay if she had a mind to stick around. She did and by the time she went back to university she had filed her first bylined piece for the paper.

'How did you find out I was in Madeira?'

'I rang the cottage then the flat; James was reluctant to tell me where you were. Am I interrupting anything by coming?'

'No.'

'Only, I know some couples like time to play away.'

'Nothing like that.' Kate thought of James going to all five days of the Lords Test; one day, long ago, had been enough for her.

'No secret lover?'

'Certainly not.'

Svetlana smiled at her mischief making.

A mongrel, mealy coloured with too large a fluffy tail curled over its back, sniffed the steps of a café across the square. It wasn't the first stray dog to come by; it lingered before turning towards their restaurant. For a while it stood eyeing the tourists sitting nearest until they shooed it away. It backed off with a quizzical expression, cocking its head to one side, then went to the side to slip in amongst the tables.

Svetlana took a piece of meat from her skewer. The dog looked at it warily, stretching forward to sniff at the offering, edged nearer, took it from her hand and gobbled the morsel. Other diners looked over with disapproval; Svetlana didn't care.

'There were a lot of stray dogs in Grozny.' The dog let Svetlana stroke its head. 'Incredible with all the shells and gunfire, always a dog trotting along going about its business, keeping alive for another day.'

'I read your dispatches.'

'Dogs, old ladies, children, all searching for food; I didn't send everything; it was too painful.'

'It was your job. Have you still got unsent copy?'

'Dear Kate, you are always an editor. I lost my laptop, more likely it was stolen. I won't go back.'

'That's between you and your new bosses. It's their loss. For my part, I'm glad.' Kate reached out and held the young woman's wrist. 'I'm happy you're safely home.'

'Perhaps I've lost my nerve.' Svetlana put her hand on Kate's. 'Come on, we need another bottle, you've drunk it all.'

'Svetlana, you've been gulping it down.'

'What the hell.' She waved at their waitress lifting the upturned bottle. 'I didn't have a single drink out there. Six months on the wagon, I've earned it.'

'You can drink at the apartment. I've got whisky, gin, wine whatever you want.'

'First we must have more champagne. Come on little dog, one more piece of meat for you.'

'Have you seen the young men over by the tree?'

'In the square?' quizzed Svetlana.

'Sitting down, drinking beer, good-looking; they've been watching you.'

'Perhaps it's you they want; an older woman. I don't want a man, not tonight. Not for a long time.'

'Is that what happened, a man?'

‘Sort of,’ she reached for the pack of cigarettes. It was empty. ‘Shit.’

‘You come here again, Madam, you like my bistro?’ The proprietor, round and contented, recognised Kate as he brought over their second bottle of champagne.

‘It was an excellent meal last night, and this evening.’

‘Your meal was good?’ he challenged Svetlana.

‘I shared it with my little friend.’ Svetlana looked the owner in the eye.

‘The dog comes every evening. Usually someone is kind to her.’

‘Does she have no home?’

‘Her home is the streets, like the others. She’s good-tempered; some are not. The authorities, they say there are too many stray dogs. They plan to round them up.’

‘And then?’

The proprietor shrugged his shoulders, put his hand to his head, his fingers in the shape of a revolver and made to fire the trigger with his middle finger.

Svetlana looked at the dog dozing at her feet. ‘Do you sell cigarettes?’

‘There’s a machine inside. But I give you ladies cigars. All my good customers I give a cigar.’

He turned away, taking the empty bottle, directing the waitress to clear their plates.

‘You don’t want a cigar, Svetlana.’

‘You told me to give up cigarettes.’

‘To give up smoking; a man would be better for you than a cigar. They’re still watching you.’

‘A cigar is better tonight; you have the men, have both of them. Then you will have a story to tell your husband. I’ll have my cigar and talk to my dog.’

The patron returned with a box of cigars of many sizes. He held it open to Kate. She declined; Svetlana chose a cheroot.

‘You will enjoy. Here, take another one for your mother.’ He bowed his head to Kate and left them.

‘Thank you,’ Svetlana laughed, ‘Mother.’

‘At least he’s made you laugh.’

Svetlana unwrapped the paper-clad cheroot, savoured it in her fingers before licking her lips and putting the dry leaf to her mouth. She rolled her lips to get comfortable with it then lit the cigar, drawing in blue smoke. Part of a bread roll was left on the table; she gave it to the dog.

The second bottle lingered while she smoked, letting a long ash accumulate. Crowds milled around the square; families in from the countryside meeting up and talking animatedly while bored children wandered off, ignored by parents. The young men decided Svetlana wasn’t interested, paid for their beers and left with a last hopeful stare in her direction.

Svetlana gazed out towards the harbour; her free hand fondling the dog’s ear.

‘If I was your editor, I would tell you to go back.’ Kate smiled, glad they were together, goading her. ‘But you were poached by the Agency so I can say what I feel as a friend.’

‘What do you feel?’

‘You haven’t told me what happened.’

‘I will. I’ve been thinking. Why don’t we adopt the dog? We can take her home with us.’

‘Back to England?’

‘Why not?’ Svetlana looked down. The dog had gone.

‘Come on, drink up. We’ll take a taxi. Tomorrow I’m going to take you on a long walk.’

‘Can’t I just sleep?’ Then she added with a laugh, ‘Mother.’

‘No you can’t and if you’re going to call me that, I’m going to mother you. You need fresh air in your lungs.’

‘I’ll walk if we can adopt my friend.’

This was the determination Kate recognised, pleased the dog had moved away.

Dappled sunlight fell onto the narrow irrigation canal as they trekked along the *Levada do Furado Trail* running along the mountain contour with the gentle flow of the channel curving across steep woodland, high above a road hair-pinning its way out of the valley. In places their path edge had fallen away; Svetlana, stretching out her arms as if she were walking a high wire, laughed at Kate’s plea for caution. At times the path tunnelled into the rock face, dripping cold showers of water as they passed through. Kate, breathless in the mountain air, struggled to keep pace.

A report rang out, echoing around the valley. Svetlana froze.

‘Thank heavens you’ve stopped. I can’t keep up with you.’

Svetlana shivered, rooted to the spot, staring at Kate. ‘What the fuck was that?’

'Something backfiring on the road, I guess.'

'It was a gun. Some bastard is shooting at us.'

'No one is shooting at us. It was a car, down below on the road. Let's have a break. I've got biscuits in my backpack.'

'It was a shot. I know a rifle when I hear it.' Svetlana couldn't move.

'It was a car, I promise.' The girl was shaking, gooseflesh on her arms, sweat on her brow. 'You should've eaten breakfast. We'll have biscuits then we can have a Poncha at the bistro where the path ends.'

'A Poncha?

'It will refresh you. It's made with rum and lemon. I'm going in front from here, to set the pace.'

Running her shower, Kate enjoyed the needling massage of water pulsing on her back, easing the ache from carrying her backpack. Stepping out into the chill of the bathroom she was glad to wrap herself in an oversized bathrobe and wander onto the balcony looking out over Funchal harbour. She lay back on a rattan steamer chair in late afternoon sun, letting her robe fall open for the last heat of the day to caress her body.

Rain clouds hung in the far distance over the Atlantic; she pulled the towelling robe together. A cruise ship blared out its baleful siren, casting off from a distant pier and setting course for tomorrow's destination.

Immersed in her book, a glass of wine beside her, Kate heard the door of the apartment. 'Is that you, Svetlana?'

'It's me.' There was the sound of steps across the wood block floor, an unfamiliar clicking with them. 'Me and my friend.'

'Svetlana, you can't.'

'I can, and I have. You're to be nice to my dog. She's come to stay.'

'Dogs are not allowed here.'

'The lady in the apartment below has two dogs and I saw another one being taken for a walk.'

'How can we feed her?'

'I'll go to the store, they have dog food and I'll buy a lead and a collar for Scruff.'

'Scruff?'

'I've wanted a dog called Scruff ever since I was a child. Kate, please? You heard what he said. They're going to be rounded up and shot.'

'Svetlana, she isn't a house dog, she's a pack animal, she lives by her wits. I can't take it back to England.'

'Not "it", this is Scruff. I've decided I'm going to stay here. I'm not going back to report on Chechnya. I'm going to find a place to live, where I can paint and look after dogs. I'm not cut out to fly all over the world, reporting on misery, always the innocent people suffering as life around them crumbles.'

'Scruff it is, but I've got to go back to the UK at the weekend. You don't really want to live here and become a dog-lady do you?'

'I do. I'll get a place to live, we both will, won't we Scruff?' Svetlana looked down. The dog wagged its too-long-curled-over-its-back-fluffy tail and Svetlana burst into tears, deep tears. Kate reached out and hugged her, wanting to ease the hurt within.

'You'll need a garden for her.'

'How long can you stay, Kate?'

‘Till the weekend.’

‘Please stay longer. If you’re here I’ll get things done.’

‘While I look after Scruff?’

‘No. I want you to help me sort myself out.’

‘You haven’t told me what happened.’

‘I’m not important. It’s all the others, the people who can’t get away.’

They ate pasta on the balcony, the sun setting into the Atlantic, Scruff seldom away from Svetlana’s side. Kate ignored the pasta shells finding their way from Svetlana’s plate to the dog, vowing to set rules in the morning. After it had grown dark Svetlana lounged back on the steamer chair and stroked the little dog by her side.

‘They won’t shoot you, Scruff; you’re safe now you live with me. The Russian Officer said I was a spy. He was going to have me shot. They shot Gorgy, my guide. Dear, sweet, Gorgy, they stripped him naked, took him out and shot him. They held my head at the window and made me watch his execution.’ The dog stared into Svetlana’s eyes, absorbing every word.

Svetlana had closed her mind to the hours after Gorgy’s death with the drunken Russian guard and the tearful teenage conscript in the stinking room. The ogling guard, his hand massaging the gaping crutch of his uniform, opening his fly to rummage inside as he told the conscript to strip off first her shirt then her trousers. The guard swore and cursed, gulping from a vodka bottle, a stream of liquid coursing down his unshaven chin. Svetlana had trembled, wanting to lash out at the conscript, disable him, and spring at the lounging figure of the guard, grab the machine pistol on the table as with trembling hands the boy fumbled with the buttons on her shirt.

The guard's head lolled back and he snored in a revolting drink-sodden sleep.

How long was it? Was it hours? It was probably minutes, even seconds. She let the conscript put his hands on her body, Svetlana forced herself to look him in the eye as his hands grew stronger, then she kicked out and he screamed, doubling up. She grabbed the automatic weapon; it went wild in her hand, the full magazine pumping into the drunken guard. She grabbed her shirt, she ran and she ran.

Kate rested her hand on Svetlana's shoulder, swallowing against the lump in her throat. The young woman rested her cheek on the comforting hand, her warm tears running down Kate's fingers. Kate bent to kiss Svetlana's cheek.

The snarling dog flew at Kate's face, its lips curled back, a tooth catching Kate's cheek before the stray turned and fled. Svetlana leapt up chasing the dog to the door.

'Let her go, Svetlana.'

The dog bolted down the stairwell.

'Svetlana, she's wild, she's not a house dog.' Kate put her hand to her bleeding cheek.

Svetlana slumped to the floor, drained of emotion.

Kate surprised herself at her strength carrying the recumbent form onto a bed. She stripped off Svetlana's clothes, worrying at the too-thin body she tucked into bed. As she closed the shutters across the window Svetlana stirred.

Kate looked at the young woman, then whispered, 'I'll book our flights to London in the morning.'

BROKEN SPACE

A salty breeze blew across sand stretching to far horizons. Kathleen watched her daughter scrape out shapes in the sand, palm trees, copying the Saharan oasis remembered from her school book.

The girl concentrated on her sandy task, ringlets of windblown hair framing her tanned face, content to play on her own, the sole child for miles in these island parts. Every school morning a car from Castletown collected Meg, bringing her home from primary school in the afternoon, a serious figure sitting alone on the back seat of the taxi. Schoolwork absorbed the child, Kathleen hoped she would to take after her grandfather who'd sailed through his exams from his schooldays to a Double First in Sciences at Cambridge before reverting to his first love: the sea.

The late-night telephone call from her mother gnawed at Kathleen's mind. It was hard to imagine her father wanting to be alone. 'Rollo' as everyone in the family, his navy colleagues and scientific peers knew him, was the comforting person they went to with their problems.

Kathleen had suggested he visit Sandiskay to recuperate; a train trek from London connecting in Glasgow for Oban before catching the twice-weekly ferry to the Outer Isles. The Island's tranquillity would ease the privation of the journey and his worries. The huge landscape had brought Kathleen to the island to paint, concerned so remote a place would not be fair to Meg, but the child revelled in their new home adopting the lilting speech of her schoolfellows, happy in the make-believe world she built around her daily play. Rollo's visit would be the chance for Meg to know her grandfather; with no man in their household there were things her daughter was missing.

'Can I have a swim, Mummy?'

'It'll be freezing.'

'It's hot.'

'Not in the sea. Just have a paddle.'

'Will you come, too?'

'I'll paddle with you; it's far too cold to swim.'

They ran down the beach together, to the foam rolling in off Atlantic breakers. Meg peeled off her clothes, dropping them, to run naked in to the sea. Kathleen, her mane of blonde hair whipping her face, her feet sucked into sand pulled by the sea edge surf, called after the child jumping through the breakers with squeals of delight. On a whim Kathleen stripped, flinging her clothes back to the dry sand and ran after her daughter in tripping bounds to plunge headlong into the breakers and embrace the child. The sea grasped her belly plucking breath from her lungs.

Panting for breath they raced together back across the beach, gathering up sandy garments, to run dripping all the way home for tea. Lambs half grown to the size of the ewes came bounding to the fence as they reached their squat slate-roofed house with its chimney, topped by a leaning cowl, bent over in winter's gales.

Rollo stood up to his journey determined to put a brave face on the anxiety lurking in his subconscious. Kathleen, who'd left Meg boarding with her school teacher, was hurt to see her father changed in spirit and physique. The man who had dominated her childhood with his jovial presence was a poor shadow of the man in her memory. They met in Glasgow, by the time their train reached Oban, Rollo was tired. He brightened as they waited on the fish quay, screaming gulls wheeling overhead to scavenge from sandwich-snacking tourists.

Rollo watched the ferry pass the point on Kerrera, always excited to see a ship come alongside. He smiled at Kathleen and squeezed her hand.

It rained for the next few days, soaking Rollo whenever he walked out from the cottage to explore their enclosure of croft land. Meg taught her grandfather to feed the hens so he could do it for her on school days. When the rain cleared they collected eggs, searching in the long grass where stubborn hens laid out, refusing to use the nest boxes in the chicken house.

Kathleen took her father on the Postbus to Castletown on his first Friday to buy waterproofs and walking boots. Once equipped his explorations took him alone onto the moor, or when Meg went with him, to the seashore, his greying hair grown long, he strode out with his granddaughter skipping along to keep pace, her yellow waterproof contrasting with the country green of Rollo's coat. They came back from their forays with stones, grasses, seaweed and shells of all colours. Meg delighted at the challenge of bringing things home and naming them from books as her grandfather watched, helping when she got stuck.

On other days, Rollo would tramp off by himself for hours at a time, trudging the machair, returning home intense and introspective. Kathleen didn't pry as they worked around the croft, hoping he would let her into his mind. Remembering her childhood, she asked him to draw with her. He soon tired of it, crumpling his paper into a ball with uncharacteristic violence. Later, Kathleen retrieved his drawing, making nothing of the puppet shapes spread-eagled across the paper like flying acrobats.

'You said you would read to me,' piped up Meg.

'Not tonight, pet,' Rollo answered with a tired smile. 'Ask your mother, she'll read to you.'

'But she's not as good as you are, Gramps. She doesn't do all the voices like you do.'

'Thank you, young madam. I'm sorry my reading isn't good enough for you.'

'You're quite good, Mummy. Gramps is best of all. He is the best reader in the whole world.'

'Not tonight, Meg, I'm going out walking.'

'In the rain?'

'Yes, and you ask far too many questions.' Rollo got up, grabbed his coat from the hook on the back of the door and stamped out of the house without a further word.

'But he promised he would read tonight.' Meg looked at the closed door, her lip trembling.

'Gramps is very tired, pet. I'll read with you,' Kathleen urged, upset to see two people she loved so unhappy.

'Don't cry, Mummy. You can read if you want, but if he's tired he shouldn't go out walking. And he didn't put on his boots.'

In the dusk when the rain had cleared, Kathleen shut up the chicken house. Rollo was sitting on a distant knoll staring into the moonlit sky. She looked out again before going to bed. He hadn't moved. He came in after three o'clock as the summer sun broke the north-eastern horizon.

'Mum phoned, she had a fright yesterday.' Kathleen told her father after breakfast. 'She was backing the car onto the street, in the mirror she caught sight of someone stepping into her path. She braked, when she got out to look there was no one there.'

'What do you mean no one was there? You said she saw someone.'

'She thought she saw someone, she looked everywhere yet there was no one to be seen. They couldn't have run away. It all happened too quickly.'

'Was it a man or a woman?'

'It was a man, a tall man.'

'What did he look like?'

'Mum said he looked American.'

'Why American?'

'She glimpsed a crew cut and a shoelace tie.'

'Oh God!' The colour drained from Rollo's face. 'It was Hank. I knew he would come.' He kicked back his chair, reaching for his coat.

'What do you mean, Dad? Who is Hank?'

'Hank was my buddy, but he's dead.' Tears ran down his ashen cheeks. 'I'm going walking.'

In the small hours Kathleen heard shouting coming from her father's room. She grabbed a gown and rushed to him. His bedclothes were thrown to the floor, his writhing body soaked in sweat.

'Hank, don't let go,' he bellowed. 'God, man hang on, get back for heaven's sake, Hank! I can't reach you.' Rollo's body arched in a spasm on the bed, his arm swept out, reaching. He grabbed hold of Kathleen's leg in a vice-like grip, she yelped at the pain, levering his fingers from her thigh. Rollo slumped back onto the bed, a frightful groan on his lips. He fell back into tortured sleep. Kathleen picked up the covers to spread over him before limping back to her bed. In the dim light of early morning she saw a livid wheal on her leg.

Over breakfast he evaded her questions. She persuaded him to take the Postbus into town to get groceries, a task he enjoyed. Rollo had tried to help around the house, he'd worked in the vegetable garden, but left the gate open for the sheep to sneak in and munch their plants. He promised Kathleen he would fix the "spinning granny", the cowl on the chimney bent over in the gales. She'd already arranged to get one of the young men to do it when haymaking was finished.

Rollo took the shopping list and set out for the Postbus. He would wait in town for the afternoon return ride home having a sandwich and a beer at The Harbour Inn. If fishermen were on the quay he could talk boats and the sea as they worked on their nets.

Kathleen needed to write down all she'd witnessed. She took a spiral-bound notebook from her desk, found a pen that worked and burst into tears, her shoulders shaking as she held her head in her hands, her hair falling over her face funnelling tears onto the blank page. What could do this to her father? Was it a diving accident? He had worked on submarines, Hank, whoever he was, had died. That she knew, and Rollo felt he was to blame. Perhaps he was.

For an hour and two coffees, she wrote down everything about her father and the pain he was enduring; by late morning she felt her burden lifting. She washed her face, brushed her hair and telephoned McPherson.

Alistair McPherson, Writer to the Signet, was the solicitor in Castletown. He needed no excuse to call on Kathleen to collect the notebook as she prepared lunch. Unmarried in his late thirties, he had few chances of meeting eligible women on the island.

Kathleen didn't want to talk about her father over cheese and home-made rolls. Alistair admired her paintings, was shown the chickens and the sheep, all given names by Meg, took her notes and promised to get back to her.

The Postbus returned without Rollo. The driver brought in Rollo's store bags with his purchases.

'They were abandoned at The Harbour Inn, he left in a hurry,' Hamish told her.

As was his custom mulling over an issue, Alistair McPherson paced to and fro in his office overlooking the harbour. The ship's chronometer on his wall showed the day was already passing five in the afternoon; the ferry would dock in an hour.

'Can you make a photocopy of these notes?' He put Kathleen's notebook on his secretary's desk.

'It'll take a wee while.'

'We must get a copy away on the steamer tonight.'

McPherson took a manila envelope from his desk and addressed it to a long-time friend from his university days: *Major Patrick Simpson, Ministry of Defence, Whitehall, LONDON.*

Kathleen telephoned with the news Rollo had gone off again, leaving his shopping in The Harbour Inn. She refused McPherson's suggestion of a search party. 'He'll come back when he wants to, it's just another sign. Something must have triggered it.'

'Kathleen, I've spoken with a contact at the MoD in London. He has access to high-ranking connections. He might be able to give us an explanation. I'm sending him a copy of your notes as I'll be in London later in the week and can meet with him. Is that alright with you?'

'If you think it will help.'

Kathleen was dozing in a chair by the dying fire when Rollo came in exhausted from his journey his mud-spattered trousers torn, his shoes soaking.

'I wish I could help you, Dad. Can't you tell me about it?'

Rollo's stare echoed his despair. 'I wish I could, dearest girl, I just don't know what it all means. I know it went wrong.'

'Who was Hank?'

'We were buddies and I let him down. He's looking for me.'

'What do you mean? You said he was dead.'

'He was in the bar at Castletown this morning.'

'He can't have been, Dad.'

'He was sitting at a table in the corner away from the door. I didn't see him come in, but he was there. Hank is a big man it couldn't have been anyone else.'

'Did you speak to him?'

'I wanted to, someone walked between us and he was gone.'

'Dad, you're imagining it.'

'The accident happened. I can't remember what or where, but it happened.'

Next morning Rollo was cheerful, as if the exchange in the small hours with Kathleen had done something to lance the ulcer of his despair.

He perked up spending the days of half term with Meg, taking her for walks along the seashore, telling her tales of the sea and of famous ships.

Kathleen found her father's body lying spread-eagled on the ground below the chimneystack with the damaged cowl. The wooden ladder, with its rungs broken, lay on the ground beside him. In Rollo's face she saw again the happy father of her childhood.

What more would Hank demand of them? Would he come for her next or, the thought hit her as if a club was swung at her head, would Hank take Meg?

The week passed in a whirl of unaccustomed events. Kathleen wanted Meg to stay with friends on the mainland, yet the child insisted she needed to go to school showing a calm acceptance of her grandfather's death that mystified Kathleen. At Meg's insistence, her grandfather Rollo, Rear Admiral Wallace Rollaston RN rtd, PhD, was buried in the clifftop cemetery, looking out to the Atlantic rollers, alongside the graves of seaman washed up on the beaches of Sandiskay from years of shipwrecks.

As the last island mourners took their leave from the wake, with Meg ready for bed, Kathleen persuaded Alistair McPherson and Moira Lindsay, Meg's schoolteacher, to stay for supper with her. She'd waited all week for the child's calm to break. She needed to speak to others over her fears.

'Shall I tell you what I've learned in London?'

'Could your MoD friend tell you much? You said it would be secret.'

'It is, but I have been able to fill in many gaps.'

'Let's have a bottle on the table?' Kathleen fetched an Island Malt from the dresser.

'A dram will be welcome.' Alistair did the honours pouring a long measure into three glasses.

'Your father was seconded to NASA, to the Starscope project. It was top-secret work. He was one of a team of military scientists who flew on a shuttle mission to position spying equipment into orbit.'

'Dad went into space! How could he not have told us?' She stared at her companions.

'A far cry from life on Sandiskay, that's for sure. Maybe it explains his preoccupation with the night sky. There was an accident. Rollo and the fellow Hank were working outside the shuttle, Hank's tether detached. In a nutshell, he floated off into space "spinning like a cartwheel" is what your father said at the inquiry. Your father's own tether mysteriously released and he was barely able to save himself. The mission was aborted and the survivors returned to Earth. A follow-up mission was able to recover Hank's spacesuit. There was no body inside.'

'It was empty?'

'This was too much for anyone to explain, they closed the file. Hank's next of kin were told he was lost, presumed drowned, while swimming after a party. The surviving crew members were brainwashed to erase the episode from their memory and given honourable discharges from their respective services.'

‘The more I hear, the more I fear Hank. I worry for Meg. It wasn’t broken rungs that killed Rollo on the ladder.’

‘Was Meg close to your father?’ Moira asked. ‘And he was known as Rollo?’

‘It’s a pet name in the family and, yes, they were close, at least in recent weeks since he’s been living with us.’

‘Meg does a lot of writing at school, sometimes exercises I set, other times her own writing. She wrote a piece after your father died. I thought she was writing about your sheep. I know she gives them all names. What Alistair has told us puts it into a different context. Is her school book in her bag?’

Kathleen fetched the school bag from its hook by the door.

‘Here it is,’ Moira paused, re-reading before she passed it over. ‘Have no fear, Meg will be alright.’

Kathleen read the page written in her daughter’s neat young handwriting.

“Hank died and his buddy Rollo was very unhappy. Now Rollo is dead and they are happy again, flying together round and around the world, amongst the stars.”

‘He told Meg things he couldn’t tell me.’ Kathleen leant back and drained her glass.

DRAWING LIFE

'Let me wipe it up.'

'I'll do it.' She padded a cloth over the spilt milk. 'What are you waiting for now?'

'I need the sugar.'

'Can you do nothing for yourself?' she spooned sugar onto his cornflakes and stalked from the room.

Harold fumbled things these days. Supermarket shopping piled up at the checkout as his fingers slipped on plastic bags finding no opening. It hadn't always been that way. At nineteen with his 'wings' stitched to his uniform by his mother, his young sister Nellie giggled as their father searched for the new pilot in his box camera viewfinder. That photograph, faded with age, hung in his bedroom, evicted from the sitting room when their mother died; Nellie said they didn't want wartime memories.

Harold treasured his memories; intense days with friends, many lost in shared adventures, then peacetime came and his flying days were done. Keeping quiet about blurred vision in his right eye wasn't an option at his commercial flying medical. Years of City commuting passed by as the staff around him grew younger and the office filled with working women until one Friday afternoon they gathered in the boardroom, there was a presentation, drinks and niblets. After the weekend he stayed at home getting in Nellie's way.

‘You’re useless, Harold.’ His sister came back with an armful of towels, ‘the bathroom floor is awash.’

This was fair comment; the bath water had sloshed over the rim. Best to say nothing and find pressing business in town, perhaps browsing in the bookshop.

Nellie kept their house spotless; there was little opportunity for it to be otherwise. If Harold moved anything, even a newspaper, his sister gathered it up and restored it to its appointed place. The only space he had to himself was his bedroom. Nellie went in there when he was out. He played a game leaving slippers toe-to-toe in the centre of the room to find them neatly paired at his bedside on return.

‘Good morning.’ He bowed his greeting to the bookshop owner, refreshed by his walk. He wasn’t useless; it was just Nellie being fussy.

In a favoured corner art books, teaching books and pictures from galleries around the world tiered up to the ceiling. Harold looked through a volume on figure drawing, starting with proportions, sketching the figure in marionette blocks, building the sketch when the shape looked right. A notice board on the wall was papered with flyers. ‘*Six life drawing classes at the Theatre Studio*’ took his eye. ‘*All welcome - whether eighteen or eighty*’.

Harold delayed telling Nellie about the classes until the evening before his first lesson. His words hung in the air.

‘Are you setting out to humiliate me?’

‘Nellie, I thought you’d be pleased. I’m doing something worthwhile.’

‘Worthwhile!’ she hissed back at him. ‘Worthwhile! Is that what you call it, sitting around with riff-raff drawing brazen women?’

'It's drawing lessons, Nellie.'

'I'll never be able to go to the theatre if people know you go there drawing those... those...' Harold waited. 'Nude women,' she spat out.

'Nellie, you've got it all wrong.'

An old biscuit tin made an excellent pencil box held shut with a thick rubber band until the band broke as the lesson finished and the contents scattered over the studio floor. Harold stooped down, the room whirled around and he lost his bearings. Shivering, sitting on the floor he tried to focus, a firm hand held his shoulder, a voice insisting he stay where he was.

'Let me pick them up.'

In a few seconds Miss Mounsley had tidied up.

'I'm sorry, Miss Mounsley. I'm causing a fuss.'

'Nonsense, and please call me Angela.'

'You're very kind, Angela. I'm holding you up.'

'Not at all, Harold, I'm not in any rush.'

'If that's so may I buy you coffee?'

'Would you like to lunch here?' Angela asked as they sat at a table in the theatre bar, stirring their too-hot coffee.

'Nellie will have my lunch on the table at one o'clock sharp. I'll be in trouble if I don't turn up,' he laughed. 'My sister isn't keen on me coming to these drawing lessons. She thinks the classes are dissolute with nude models.'

'Have you shown her your drawings?'

'She won't look at them.'

'That's a pity, they're good.' Angela paused, 'I've been spying over your shoulder.'

Harold was late for lunch but didn't say a word to Nellie of his meeting with Angela Mounsley, or of his dizzy turn. It was five days before he told her he would be having lunch at the theatre after his next drawing lesson.

After lunching on tortellini, a green bean salad with black olives and a glass of Pinot Grigo at the theatre, they walked along the river embankment stopping to sit on a bench and watch boys fish in the muddy water. When he got home Harold told Nellie he'd been invited to tea with a friend from the drawing class.

Angela had asked them both; she was not disappointed when he came alone.

A silver framed sepia photograph of a young man in the high-buttoned tunic uniform of the Royal Flying Corps in the Great War stood on a bureau, three Remembrance Day poppies stuck out from behind its frame. Harold couldn't read the legend underneath the photo, but saw two dates cutting short a young man's life. Angela was proud of the great-uncle she'd never known who'd flown bi-planes in the generation before Harold.

Angela and Harold planned an adventure. He wanted to visit the airfield in Suffolk where his squadron was based before they were posted overseas. He was disappointed Nellie would never go with him.

'I could drive you, better still, we can use trains.'

'Trains would be fun and a taxi from Ipswich.' Harold remembered many late-night journeys back to the base.

The taxi dropped them, then waited by two rusting wire mesh gates across the one-time airfield entry, one bolted down, the other wide open. A concrete roadway, edged with dandelions stretched into grassland; in the distance tractors worked in tandem.

A large agricultural shed stood near dilapidated concrete buildings. A skylark sang an endless trill high in the air, unseen by Harold's watering eyes, blinking into the blue glare. Uncut grass swayed gently in a rolling breeze, one tractor toiled on loading from a silage harvester, another tractor trundled over the open land towing its high-sided trailer, hanging back, ready to take its place in their agricultural dance.

Angela linked arms strolling towards the concrete building. Harold looked around, his eyes shaded by the brim of his panama.

'There were huts, accommodation huts, freezing in winter's sleet off the North Sea, stifling in summer despite windows and doors propped open.'

'Is it familiar?'

'Not really, the huts were in rows and there were high camouflage nets for aircraft outside the hangars; the airstrip ran east to west with the cross runway running towards that wood.' He pointed toward the trees. 'I wasn't the only one to clip the tops. It wasn't an easy take-off.'

They strolled on, thistledown rolling along the roadway, the smell of cut grass wafting on the wind.

'I recognise this.' They stood by the opening into the concrete building, no door, just an entry into darkness. Harold peered in, wanting to go further, uncertain what he might find. A rusted fire extinguisher lay on its side, water dripped from the ceiling, a stalactite of leached deposit marking the leak's age.

'Shall we go in? I've got a torch in my handbag.'

'It might not be pleasant inside.'

'Nonsense; we must go in now we're here.'

'I never thought to bring a torch.'

Angela laughed. 'Most women have a torch in their handbag.' She led the way in, stepping carefully, breathing the dank air of the deserted building, reaching her hand back to guide Harold.

At the top of a staircase a metal door swung open onto a long flat with broken windows looking out across the one-time airfield. Vandals had been in, cigarette packets were cast around and a fire had been lit against one wall. A notice, peeling from the wall, listed assembly stations and, mounted outside the central window, there was a rusted iron triangle; a metal bar lay on the floor.

Angela picked up the bar, leant from the vacant window frame and tapped the triangle. The drone of the tractors rumbled on; she hit the metal harder, its first quiet clanging built up as she beat the triangle.

The call came flooding back across the years. Young pilots sitting in armchairs dragged out onto the grass, leaping up, discarding lit pipes and cold utility tea to run to the waiting planes.

'I'm sorry. I shouldn't have done that.'

His faraway eyes broke into a smile; reaching out he hugged her. 'I don't know where the last sixty years have gone.' He kissed her forehead and looked into eyes filled with happiness. Their lips touched.

The Merry Harriers had a good crowd in for lunch. Harold ordered double gin and tonics from the barmaid, she pointed to the blackboard menu listing meat, fish and pasta dishes, promising to be over to take their order.

'Do you remember this bar?'

'It's changed. There were two bars in those days, not this large space, no food other than a jar of pickled eggs on the counter, sawdust on the public bar floor, perhaps lino on this side, no carpets, gas lamps and a tap room where the beer barrels stood on trestles. The entrance wasn't there, it opened off the road in those days.'

A noisy group across the room, teenage girls and young men in leathers, crash helmets on the floor, jarred against the rural quiet of lunchtime eating. The landlord looked at them from the bar. The bikers didn't give a damn, uneasy glances came from munching diners around the room.

The waitress warned their plates, heaped with game pie, were hot as she placed a basket of plastic sauce sachets, coloured to signal content, onto the table.

'It's not easy to enjoy lunch in the company of that loud group.' Harold looked across the bar.

'Should have seen Alfie, blasting up the bleedin' bypass, went like fuck he did.'

'I've got used to it, Harold. Sometimes teaching in school the language is dire, and from girls, too.'

'Pipe down, can't you Frankie, they're all staring.'

'If only they were a bit quieter.'

'If the tossers want to stare they can. We've as much soddin' right to be here as those wankers.'

The landlord hesitated.

Harold stood up, stretching to his full height. He'd had trouble folding himself into the cramped fighter cockpit yet the discomfort was worth it for the thrill and beauty of a machine flying at twelve thousand feet. Angela reached out to hold him back. He walked across the room.

'Excuse me, young man. There are ladies here, would you keep a civil tongue, or be silent.'

Frankie was astounded. Staring at Harold, he rose up a broad figure in his leathers, but giving away inches to the older man. 'And who the hell are you?'

Harold's cheeks reddened, he surveyed the young man's group, looking each person in the eye before clasping Frankie's arm, 'I'll tell you who I am.' He led the young biker to the bar. 'Landlord, would you be good enough to pass down that photograph behind the bar.'

The landlord looked at the two men. He didn't want trouble.

'Please, the photograph.'

A black and white picture, cobwebs falling from its frame, was placed on the bar. Harold pointed to a fresh-faced youngster at one end of the row in the picture.

'Bradbury, "Kipper" Bradbury, from New Zealand, he was twenty-one when he was shot down over Kent. He lived for three weeks, massively burned. Mercifully he died.'

Harold's finger picked out the next man in the group of young airmen and women standing laughing to the camera outside The Merry Harriers of long ago. 'Charlie Light, credited with downing ten enemy aircraft, went missing over Northern France, his plane was never found.'

His finger moved again. 'Fred Santer, a wonderful pilot, finished a mission at midday, rode off on his BSA motorcycle, going home for his wedding on Tyneside, hit by a lorry on the Great North Road and killed instantly.'

The bar was silent, everyone straining to hear the insistent tones of the tall military figure.

'Anne and Julie Wilkins, sisters,' his finger encompassed two of the three women in the photo, smiling happily to the camera. 'They were duty WAAFs on the night of the first bombing raid on the airfield, both killed with a direct hit on the Ops Room.'

Again his finger moved, 'William Kidd, from the United States, didn't wait for the Americans to join the war, had flown for a circus and delivered mail all over the States, lied about his age in case he was thought too old for operations. He won a DFC and bar, you can guess his nickname. When his fighter was hit over France he bailed out and was machine-gunned hanging from his parachute.' Harold paused, memories buzzing in his mind. 'The others survived.'

Harold still held the young man's arm; he looked him in the eye. 'We drank in this pub when we could get away from duty, this was home to us.' He pointed to the tall young flyer at the further end of the row. 'I was lucky. I survived. That's who I am.'

Frankie stared, the disdain of the whole room bearing down. A person clapped, then another, until a burst of applause filled the bar.

'You'd better clear out and take the others with you,' the landlord at last came to life.

'No, if I may, Landlord, I would like to buy Frankie and his companions, a drink, soft drinks as I imagine they'll be getting back on those powerful machines I saw in the car park. I guess, Frankie, you know more about machines and engines than ever I did. You would have been one of us if you'd been my age. We were pretty wild at times and often in this pub.'

Drinks were placed on the bar; Harold fumbled in his purse to find the coins to pay; he handed his purse to Frankie. 'Here, you find the right money.'

The landlord held up a hand. 'They're on the house.'

Harold crossed over to Angela sitting with tears rolling down her cheeks. 'Don't worry, Angela. Back to our lunch; I see there's an exciting pudding menu.'

JANET'S CHRISTMAS LIST

Her list was getting longer. Janet had a thing about lists with several on the go at any time, for shopping, for household chores, even a garden list. Harry teased her and forgot things he was meant to be doing, Janet always remembered.

She'd made lists since her schooldays, rebuked standing at her desk, as an example to the class over a schoolbook left at home. Miss Brook – 'Babbling Brook' to generations of school girls – lectured Janet and the class to make lists of things to do. From that day Janet kept lists, at college, at work and at home. There was little that Miss Brook had taught her that had endured into later life, other than her daily updating of lists.

This was her Christmas list for Aunt Lilly's stay and for festivities on the day; it wasn't shaping well. Janet couldn't concentrate, she felt a cold coming on, Harry was late from work on the evening they had set aside for decorating the tree, Suzanna was being difficult sulking in her room with the sound system booming and Jack was raiding the fridge to make one of his boy-sandwiches.

'Get the phone, Jack.'

'I'm busy.'

'Do I have to do everything?'

'You like doing everything.'

'You are on thin ice, young man. Hello... oh, it's you, where on earth are you...? What do you mean come and fetch you, can't you walk?' Janet sighed and made a face.

'Are there no taxis?'

Jack stopped in mid bite.

'I'm not feeling in the best of health myself. If you've been in the pub, I'll...' She put the phone down, took the car keys off a hook and picked up her handbag. 'Feed the dog Jack and clear up the mess you are making. I've got to fetch your father from the station. He says he is ill.'

Next morning, Harry was unable to stir from his bed. His only contribution to family social activity was to insist his aunt couldn't stay with them over Christmas. She would have to go to his sister's. Janet ignored this decree; Aunt Lilly would already be setting out for Waterloo to catch her train.

The awful truth was that whatever Harry was suffering was spreading. Janet's head was spinning, she found it hard to concentrate on anything and by midday decided to delegate the task of meeting Aunt Lilly to the children.

'She'll have luggage.'

'Don't argue, Suzanna. There's a twenty pound note on the dresser. You can both walk to the station and take a taxi back.'

'What if it costs more than that?'

'It won't and you can keep the change. I'm going upstairs to lie down. Don't forget, half past three, the train from London.

'It's bound to be late. Do I have to go?'

'You are both going and you are to be polite to your great-aunt. It's good of her to come all this way to stay with us over the holiday.'

'She's old, like she's out of the ark. I'm hungry, when's lunch.'

'Jack, one day you'll be old, now make your own lunch.'

'Give us another note and we can go to the pizza place,' Jack smiled.

'No way, I'm not being seen in there with you.' His sister glared at the boy.

'I'm going upstairs to bed.' Janet clutched a handkerchief to her running nose and left the children in the kitchen.

The train was late, twenty minutes late, a crowd of travellers stepped down and Lilly was nowhere to be seen.

'Suzanna, can it be you?' a familiar voice spoke behind her.

'Great-Aunt Lilly, I thought you must have missed the train.'

'It was packed, thank heavens I booked my seat. You must call me Lilly now you are so grown up. Are you on your own?'

'Jack's gone to grab a taxi. Mother and Father are malingering at home, saying they are ill.'

'So we will be doing the Christmas cooking; that'll be fun, Suzanna.'

'Hardly; we'd better go out to a hotel.'

'Dear me, no. I'm sure the two of us can cope with Jack's help.'

'Jack's useless, he'll muck about.'

On cue, her brother weaved his way through the crowd of departing passengers pulling bags and talking with family greeters making their slow progress away from the platform. Jack clutched a half-eaten beef burger in his hand. 'There aren't any.'

'Hello Jack, where have you been hiding.'

'She sent me to get a taxi and there aren't any.'

'We can walk then, it won't take long and I've been sitting down all the way from London.'

'It's miles to walk; Mum gave us twenty quid for the taxi fare and we can keep the change, half each.'

'So if we walk we can split the twenty pounds three ways and we'll each have more money,' the old lady smiled at her young welcoming party as they tried to catch up with her arithmetic.

'What about your suitcase?'

'It has wheels, Jack. I'm sure a strong lad like you will find it no problem and I might forego my six pound sixty-six to split between you both. It can be our secret.'

'Suzanna has to do her share with the suitcase.'

'Perhaps Suzanna will carry my spare coat and umbrella.'

'Certainly, Lilly.'

'That's not fair, and it is Great-Aunt Lilly to you.'

'It is for you dear brother, isn't it Lilly?'

There was no sound in the house, not even a radio playing. The kitchen was as the children had left it, unwashed plates stacked in the sink, an unwrapped sliced loaf on the table with open jars of peanut butter, marmite and jam beside butter in a dish smeared with all three. Lilly took off her coat and set to tidying the kitchen. Jack was dispatched to take his great-aunt's suitcase to the spare bedroom and Suzanna to check on her parents. She reported both to be asleep, breathing loudly, with a pile of used paper handkerchiefs on each side of the bed.

Lilly had found Janet's list, she'd checked the fridge and the larder. She asked Suzanna where the nearest shops were.

'You'll have to drive to get to the supermarket.'

'I gave up driving years ago. We passed several local shops on the way from the station.'

Jack ran into the kitchen. 'Are they dead, they're not moving?'

'Dead people don't snore, stupid.'

'Don't worry, Jack. You come with me to the shops and I'll add cold and flu medicines to the list.'

'I'm hungry.'

'We can go to the cafe I saw on the way over here. Will you come with us, Suzanna?'

'No way... I mean, I'm not hungry, Lilly. I have things to do.'

'Like luv-texting Billy boy, I bet.'

'Shut up, twerp.'

'You stay here then Suzanna, and when your parents wake, take them up weak tea and paracetamol. Jack, you come with me to carry the shopping.'

By six o'clock next evening, Christmas Eve, the tree, so dismally dressed before Aunt Lilly's arrival, was dominating the sitting room with a cascade of decorations, glittering strands of silver and gold, surrounded by brightly wrapped presents. There were logs piled up beside a rouging fire after Lilly had rung a log man found in the Yellow Pages and told him in firm tones the first week of January was no good and he had better come with a trailer load without delay or not at all.

Janet and Harry had been persuaded to stay in bed, Toby, the dog, was fed, the larder stocked up ready for Christmas morning, high tea had been served and washed up and the three of them, Lilly, Suzanna and Jack, were sitting in front of a blank television screen having found no programme they could agree on after Lilly had insisted they watch the King's College Carol Service.

'Shouldn't you take Toby out into the garden, Jack? He's hardly been out all day.' Suzanna wanted to be alone with Lilly; she didn't want to upset her, but her boyfriend, Billy, had texted to ask her to come for Christmas lunch with his folks.

Jack was tearing strips from the newspaper and crumpling the shreds into balls.

'Do you have to do that all the time?'

'Yes, sister dear, I juz have to do it.'

Lilly got up to look at the shelves of DVDs. 'There must be something here we can all enjoy.'

'It's mostly Dad's obsession with Star Wars and Tolkien.'

'Sense and Sensibility?'

'That's Mum's, all the costume dramas are hers and the musicals.'

'Which are yours, Suzanna?'

'None of those, mine are in my room and never allowed out.'

'Here's one of my favourite films, we could all enjoy this – Mrs Henderson Presents.'

Suzanna stared at her great-aunt; Jack bored with screwing up balls of torn newspaper was flicking them into a wicker waste paper basket. 'What does she present?'

'Burlesque, Jack, at The Windmill Theatre in London, it was a very famous venue in the years before and during the Second World War.'

'We're doing that in history, sounds too much like homework.'

'The Windmill, Jack?'

'No, the war: Dunkirk, Battle of Britain and the Blitz.'

'Lilly, you do know what went on at The Windmill, have you seen the film?'

'Oh yes, Suzanna, I've got the DVD and I watch it time and again. I know The Windmill; it was my first job.'

'Job at 't mill. Did'st thou make loaves 'ot bread, our Lillian?'

'Shut up, Jack.'

'I only asked.'

'Don't look so surprised, Suzanna.'

'Were you an usherette?'

'No, dear, it was after Mrs Henderson's days, it was in Mr Vivian van Damm's ownership just after the war in 1946. There were a lot of famous people performing at The Windmill after the war: Peter Sellers, Harry Secombe, Jimmy Edwards, Tony Hancock, Bruce Forsyth, lots of stars. I was a dancer and often a tableau vivant as we called the poses.'

'You were a Windmill Girl, Lilly?'

'Yes Suzanna, and very proud to have been one; I was seventeen, not much older than you, but I told them I was nineteen, jobs were hard to find and the one thing I was good at was dancing. I suppose you could say I ran away to the theatre after the worst family Christmas I've ever had. Mother and Father had split up that year; she'd taken your grandfather, he was only nine, away to spend Christmas with her sister and my older brother, Jack, had been shot down over Germany. He never came back. It seemed to be the end of family life and I found myself a new home, The Windmill Theatre.'

'I didn't know you had a brother.'

'Yes, he would have been your great-uncle.'

'Was I named after him?'

'You were.'

'Cool, and what's a Windmill Girl?'

'Is that a bottle of sherry I see on the sideboard, dear?'

Suzanna, unsure where the conversation was heading, went over to the bottles her father had stacked on the dresser. 'This one?' she held it up. 'It says Amontillado.'

'That will do nicely. Will you have a glass with me, Suzanna?'

'You bet,' Jack jumped up from his seat.

'Only a thimble full for you, young man. The smaller ones with stems, dear,' she added as Suzanna surveyed the glasses in the cupboard.

'These?'

'That's right; now let's watch Mrs Henderson and I can tell you all about The Windmill. I've checked nothing is forgotten on your mother's Christmas list; we are now ready for a proper Christmas. We'll have to take lunch and the crackers upstairs with the invalids in their bedroom, but we can have our Christmas tea downstairs and you can ask Billy to come over, Suzanna.'

‘Can I really? That’s mega.’

‘Yuck, must she?’

‘Is that you volunteering to do the washing-up, Jack?’

ISLAND SUMMER

The boys were stretched back on the heather, spotting the trails from airplanes outward bound over the Atlantic. There was no school today and there would be no more school on the island for these two lads. In three weeks they would be weekly boarders at the mainland Academy.

Willie sat up, screwing his eyes against the glare looking out across The Sound to the pattern of fishing vessels and beyond to the grey outline of Argyll, his lips stained purple from berries.

'Give us a go of your coke, Andy.'

'Not till lunchtime.'

'You can have a biscuit,' said Willie, 'anyway it is lunchtime,' and he grabbed for the carrier bag.

Andy knew his friend too well and in a flash had rolled out of reach.

'I'm bored.'

'Suppose we could do whatever we wanted, what would you do?'

'We could be a secret gang of spies.'

Andy reached into a pocket and pulled out a piece of paper and the stub end of a pencil. He tore the paper in half and gave a piece to Willie.

'We'll both think up something to do and write it down. We'll have to share the pencil.'

Willie wandered down to the burn to scoop up peaty water. Andy went over to a deserted bothy with no roof.

After the boys exchanged their slips of paper there was silence.

'We can't do this, Willie.'

'We can, my brother says she does.'

'She does what?'

'She has a bath with the window wide open. I heard him saying so to Cronin.'

If Willie's brother had said so to Cronin, then Andy knew it was a fact. On Willie's paper was written the challenge: *"Spy on Mrs Mermagen in her bath"*.

Willie was unbelieving of Andy's note. It read: *"Rob a bank"*.

'But there is no bank,' protested Willie.

'I mean a mainland bank. We'll go to Locharbon. There are lots of banks there.'

'How do you know?'

'My father goes to the bank when he's on the mainland.' Andy had never been to a bank with his father.

Mrs Mermagen was the doctor's sister, all the children on the island thought her beautiful. An artist, she came to live on the island a year back and every week she came to the school to teach drawing. She sang songs as she drew while her wee daughter, Abigail, played on the floor. There was no Mr Mermagen. Willie said he'd been murdered. Andy knew he was making that up.

Willie's brother had been on the hill one day looking for a peregrine's nest on the rock face and had seen a shadowy figure through his binoculars at the open bathroom window. Willie's brother had whispered this information to Cronin not knowing his young brother was listening.

The doctor's garden harboured the only apple tree on the island, a favoured secret attraction for boys on autumn days. If they were able to climb onto the roof of the old greenhouse they hoped they would be able to see into the bathroom.

The bank was a bigger problem.

'Why did you put that down?' puzzled Willie.

'I saw this film on the telly. You walk in, give the bank clerk a note and he gives you the money.'

Willie had to admit, it didn't sound difficult.

They tossed a two-penny bit. They would go to Locharbon the next day.

The boys were at the pier to watch the ferry dock. Cars drove cautiously off the landing ramp while the gangway was manoeuvred into position by the pier master's staff, allowing a line of foot passengers to come ashore.

Neither of the boys bought a ticket. They mingled with the crowd struggling aboard with cases while the crew busied themselves getting ready to sail.

As soon as they got to the mainland, Andy went to a shop and bought a postcard. It had a picture of a highland cow; he said this didn't matter. At the post office he used a pen on a chain to write his message in his best handwriting. Willie thought he should have used his left hand and written in wobbly capitals.

The message read:

"EXCUSE ME,

CAN WE HAVE TEN POUNDS, PLEASE?

THANK YOU".

The problem was not to find a bank, rather which to choose. Andy gripped Willie's arm and guided his companion into the nearest stone-fronted building.

They were at the back of a queue. The lady at the front was telling the man behind the counter she had been on her holiday, but it rained. Willie glanced up, then at Andy clutching his postcard. Everyone was holding a small book, everyone except them. Above the counter was a sign:

THE ARGYLL
PROVIDENT ASSOCIATION

He nudged Andy's arm. 'This isn't a bank,' he whispered.

The queue moved forward, Willie stayed rooted to the floor. Andy looked at him then at the sign. They turned and made for the door where an assistant was changing the sign to read: *CLOSED*.

'Remember, boys, it's early closing today.'

The boys wandered along the street looking into shops, their doors shut, the three banks and the provident society now silent behind stout doors. An amusement arcade was open, but the manager could spot boys without money to spend. He moved them on.

The steamer let its siren blast, Andy and Willie ran to the pier and made it just as the last of the passengers were going aboard.

They spent the crossing on deck. Andy tore up the postcard with the picture of the highland cow, letting the scraps spiral down into the ship's wake.

Next morning, Willie called at his friend's house. Andy came out with two bacon butties and, giving one to his pal, they set off at a brisk pace. The boys walked past their old school lying empty as a car came towards them; the doctor waved.

'Glad he's out,' said Willie. 'We can go in the front gate.'

'No, best go over the wall. Spies never go in the front gate.'

Willie didn't argue.

The boys climbed the wall and with the garden deep in summer growth it was easy to creep unobserved round to the greenhouse. There were panes of glass missing, others broken; a few tomato plants, short of water, grew inside twisting through an old grape vine.

The bathroom window was open, they could hear singing as a waft of steam came curling out into the sunny morning.

Willie climbed onto a water butt and reached up to the greenhouse roof. Andy went back to the wall to stand guard.

Willie worked his way up the wooden eave, taking care to put no weight directly onto the glass panes. At the top there was a pointed finial, he reached out and pulled himself up to the highest point, sitting up so his viewpoint was as high as he could make it. Willie heard the bath water released gurgling down the cast iron drainpipe, an arm reached up holding a towel.

Andy watched Willie trying to stand on the greenhouse roof as a large van swept around the corner, stopping in front of the doctor's house, giving several blasts from its horn.

It was the Travelling Bank over on the morning ferry from the mainland. People emerged from houses as Andy whistled a warning to his fellow spy.

Hearing the hooter, Mrs Mermagen looked out of the window. Willie had never in all his life seen so beautiful a sight as Mrs Mermagen at the window, her torso the same sunburned brown as her arms. Willie's mouth gaped wide open and his knees shook.

'Why Willie Campbell, I do declare you're spying on me,' she laughed in surprise, lifting her hands to cover her bosom.

People milled around the bank bus. The teller opened the doors and was starting to serve his customers.

Willie lost his balance. With a shattering crash, he fell through the greenhouse roof.

Mrs Mermagen screamed.

The bank was forgotten as the crowd ran from the road into the doctor's garden.

There was a lot of blood. Cushioned by the vine's encircling boughs, no bones were broken. Prompted either by shock or good judgement, Willie fainted.

By chance, the doctor returned home as the crowd surged into his garden and, making certain there was no serious damage, he had the still unconscious Willie carried into the surgery and placed on the couch. Andy crept into the room and saw his friend lying senseless. A warm arm went around his shoulders to comfort him. He turned to find Mrs Mermagen behind him.

'Is he dead?'

She smiled down. 'No, he's just fainted. He'll be alright.'

The doctor soon had Willie awake, his cut arms cleaned, a few stiches in place and finished with bandages.

'Now then Willie, what on earth was going on?' demanded the doctor.

'Oh, I saw it happen,' said his sister.

Willie thought it best to play faint again. Andy looked at his feet.

'He was helping himself to tomatoes when he fell through the greenhouse roof; I told you the greenhouse was dangerous.

Willie knew at that moment he loved Mrs Mermagen, even as much as he loved his mother.

Leaving them alone in the surgery, the doctor promised to take the boys home in his car. Andy pushed his hand into his pocket and pulled out something for Willie to see.

'Where did you get that?' demanded Willie.

'From the bank, when they all went to see what had happened.'

'You robbed the bank?'

Andy smiled. He wasn't going to tell Willie the ten pound note had fallen on the ground in the confusion of the accident. After a pause, he asked, 'Did you see Mrs Mermagen in her bath?'

Willie nodded.

It was good being members of a secret gang.

EMILY'S BEQUEST

A place for everything and everything in its place, if Emily was told this once in her childhood she heard it a thousand times. Her mother need not have worried, Emily was tidy by nature and years later her flat reflected the neatness of her ways.

It was the reason Emily found it hard when anyone came to visit. Things would be put away in wrong places as guests fussed around wanting to help. So Emily lived in a flat too small to have people to stay.

It wasn't a dislike of others, she was proud of the ever-larger number of nieces and nephews, then great-nieces and great-nephews, not to mention the godchildren and their offspring, she accumulated in her long life.

'I've come to visit Miss Pearson.' Rachael, weary from her journey across London, stood at the hospital reception desk.

'Ward seven.'

She followed the signing through twists and turns along bewildering corridors until finding a door marked *Ward Seven - Duty Sister.*

'Miss Emily Pearson, she's my aunt?'

Rachael was shocked to see the frail old lady the nurse woke. For a moment she thought it was the wrong bed. It was only six weeks since she had seen her aunt, very much her usual self, over tea and cakes at Cawardine's Tea Room.

'Emily, Rachael has come to see you.' The nurse gently brought the old lady out of her sleep.

'Hello, Aunt Emily.'

'Have a sip of water, dear.' The nurse helped her patient take a mouthful of water. The old lady perked up trying to focus on her visitor.

'Aunt Emily, it's Rachael. I've dropped by to see you.'

'I don't know why I'm here, dear. They're very nice, but they don't know what's wrong with me. I think I will go home tomorrow.'

'You had a fall, Aunt Emily.'

'I don't think so, dear.' The old lady reached a frail hand toward the cupboard by her bed. 'Can you find it for me?'

'What do you want, Emily?'

'There's a key. In my bag, can you get the key for my strongbox? And the list; I want you to give them out for me?'

Rachael was puzzled, but tiredness overtook the old lady sinking back into her dreams.

Rachael didn't sleep until the small hours of the night, tired from her journey back to her South London home through rush-hour crowds.

Next morning the Duty Sister rang to let her know.

'What do you think Emily meant about a list?' she asked her cousin when they met in Emily's flat the day after the funeral. 'There was no list in her bag.'

'Perhaps there are things she has left in her will.' Alice looked at the photos of long ago on the walls and the faded furniture.

Rachael was glad she was not alone at the flat. Someone else's place, their familiar home-ground for years, until one day they don't return and their possessions, collected over years, lose connection becoming bric-a-brac, barely worth a glance.

'I can't see any strongbox.' Rachael had been looking through the drawers of Emily's desk. Glancing across the room she noticed the base of a black metal document chest, covered with a fitted cushion she had taken to be a low seat by the window. They took the cover away and the key fitted neatly into the lock.

'It doesn't look promising.' Alice pulled out years of bank statements in plastic folders, old cheque stubs, a current chequebook and two of their aunt's old passports with photos taken in Emily's twenties and thirties.'

'She said something about two books.' Rachael turned over the remaining papers in the strongbox finding a bunch of keys. 'I guess these are for her cupboards.' Underneath everything there were two sturdy books with leather-bound spines, reinforced corners and marbled covers. The smaller was an index book.

'No wonder she never forgot a birthday.'

All the extended family were listed, page by page, name by name; dates of birth, even christening, confirmation and marriage dates. Then under each was their postal address, some with many changes and none deleted.

Rachael thumbed quickly through to find her name. After schools there were addresses for the hall of residence at university, a string of digs and forgotten flats before her matrimonial homes, the first a cramped flat, the second reflecting growing prosperity. 'Everywhere I've lived is here.'

The other book, an old-fashioned foolscap cashbook, listed all the cousins and godchildren again, but under every name a list of presents for birthdays and Christmas, with a cost in the final column, the early entries in shillings and pence.

'Emily never gave presents to anyone. Cards every year; never presents,' said Rachael, turning the pages. She found the page headed with her name. Her first birthday was marked 'knitted mittens' with the cost left blank. As she grew older the entries grew with her. At six there was a skipping rope for two shillings and sixpence, by nine a four-shilling bicycle bell. At thirteen it was riding gloves for eleven and sixpence and at eighteen a pair of stockings. The last birthday recorded was her twenty-first with a ten-guinea necklace. Her only other entry was a set of mother-of-pearl handled fruit knives for her wedding.

It was all make-believe: Aunt Emily had never given her any of these things.

They looked up the page for Alice and a similar catalogue of phantom gifts leading to her twenty-first birthday. Her list finished with a Wedgwood teapot for her wedding.

Rachael found her children's pages, more mystery lists with higher prices and in decimal currency. The pencil cases and puzzles of her youth had given way to Action Men, television toys and tapes of pop songs.

Alice boiled a kettle. They drank tea while thumbing further through the book, each page carefully totalled at its foot.

'It's sad to think of Aunt Emily sitting alone making up these lists thinking of our birthdays and Christmases.' Rachael stirred her cup. 'I wish I'd seen more of her, done more with her.'

‘We’d better go through her wardrobes next to see what clothes and stuff she left,’ said Alice getting to her feet. ‘Throw old clothes away, good ones can go to charity shops.’

‘I expect everything is old. Emily didn’t keep up with fashion, maybe they’ll suit a vintage boutique.’

Alice picked up the bunch of keys and went through to the bedroom.

‘Heavens above come and look at this, Rachael.’

The linen press doors were open, Alice, open-mouthed, was looking at its contents. ‘Look at it all.’ Neatly wrapped brown paper parcels nestled on the shelves.

The cousins tried more keys in cupboards and drawers, every time they were greeted by wrapped parcels.

‘There are hundreds of them.’ Each drawer had labels with a name and every parcel was tagged. ‘This is marked for me.’ Gingerly Rachael picked up a small package dated, Christmas 1951. She carried it through to the sitting room and looked in the leather-backed ledger, tracing down the list with her fingers.

Christmas 1951 - Conway Stewart fountain pen - 7/6.

With an unsteady hand, she undid the red string and green crepe paper inside the brown paper postal wrapping. Immaculate in its original box, she found a Conway Stewart fountain pen. ‘Alice, this is brand new yet more than fifty years old. I so wanted a pen like this when I was ten.’

They checked through their find realising every present listed in the cashbook was in the cupboards or drawers, carefully wrapped, precisely labelled and never sent. All in the mint condition they were the day Emily bought them, toys in original boxes, books in their covers; everyday things marking childhood and teenage times over the past sixty years. After years without presents Aunt Emily had left them all a legacy to remember; a token of the commonplace much sought after by collectors.

Alice looked up from the drawer marked with her name. 'Once, when I was a kid, we had a fracas at home about presents. Father told me a cautionary tale of his sister Emily never giving presents. The two of them had a childhood argument over a present she had given him. In a fit of pique, he broke it and she vowed never to give anything to anybody again as they wouldn't look after it.'

'And once she'd decided she couldn't stop because she would look after them better than us,' suggested Rachael.

'And it's true. Most of these things would have been smashed or thrown away years ago.'

'And there are no lists or drawers marked for her brothers.'

'Dear Aunt Emily, she tried to tell me; she just passed over her key and now it's too late to thank her.'

CONKERING DAYS

The train slowed for Shedbury Parva. Henry Huntington stirred in the comfort of his first class seat, surreptitiously spreading out his belongings across the table. Another hour and he would be in London. The Underground to the City for lunch and an afternoon meeting before the journey home. Perhaps he would treat himself and take a taxi. On the few times Henry went to London on business he relished privileges earned over many years, chief of these was to travel First Class.

The ironwork lattice of a defunct gas holder stood out against the rain-soaked sky, in the town beyond the station the mass of Shedbury Abbey stirred uneasy memories of school days, of bitter cold winter and sweltering uniformed summer terms long ago. Henry buried himself behind *The Times*, reading the list of Bolivian Coffee Futures, pushing his briefcase across the table.

A crackle of announcements came over the platform loudspeakers and his defences were breached. A dishevelled man, much his own age, breathing noisily from his exertion, slumped into the seat across the table getting up again as the train started out of the station to lean unsteadily against the seatback taking off his mackintosh coat; he stuffed it untidily onto the luggage rack.

'That's better,' the man announced to the carriage at large resuming his place. 'I thought I was going to miss the train.'

Henry Huntington looked up from his paper; he'd read as far as the Calcutta Jute Prices. There was a familiarity about the face opposite, reflected in the man's gaze. Their mutual glance would have gone without remark had their paths crossed in any other part of the country. As the train gathered speed from the town of shared schooldays the connection was made.

'Huntington. "Haughty" Huntington isn't it?' Recognition broke across the man's face.

It jarred for Henry to hear the loathed schoolboy nickname thrown off with his uniform the day he left Shedbury and the rest of his life began. He couldn't put any name to the face pressing toward him, but he remembered the person. He was a large man and had been a large child, much heavier than others of his age, always lingering at the back of the crocodile walking in pairs from the school to the Abbey for Sunday services.

'Fancy meeting you, Haughty; do you live around here?'

'No. I pass through on the train from time to time.'

'First time I've been back in years; the school is all flats now, old people's flats.'

Why did he have to tell the whole carriage? The man's raincoat was creased, hardly surprising from the way he bundled it up dirty and torn, his shirt no better, a loose tie, his top button missing, he was unshaven and his thin hair stuck up at odd angles; hardly a first-class passenger.

'I'm glad I've met up with you, Haughty.' The man looked with an unblinking stare, adding after a pause, 'there are things you never forget from those days.'

It would be ungracious to say nothing. 'You're not from around here, then.' Henry remembered there had been a cousin at the school, an older cousin.

'I'm a bit of a wanderer,' his fellow traveller announced for the whole carriage to hear. 'Lived abroad a long time; on my own now, children grown up and I'm divorced from the little lady.'

Henry was unsure whether to congratulate him on his grown-up children or to commiserate over his divorce.

'I say, Haughty.'

Henry cringed.

'Do you know the playing fields have gone? They've built houses all over them.'

'That happened years ago.'

'I didn't know. Bit of shock, I wanted to see the cricket field. I scored a century in a match there once.' The man looked genuinely disappointed. 'Just wretched houses everywhere, you can't even tell where the cricket square was.'

'I'm sorry.' Henry suppressed a smile, imagining this gross and ageing man wandering around private suburban gardens, trying to find the place where his cricketing prowess had flowered decades ago.

'It shouldn't have been allowed. Some jerry-builder ripped the school off, I'll bet.'

'The school went bust.'

'I knew the school had closed, but the playing fields.'

'Probably an Old Boy built the houses,' ventured Henry.

'That's rotten; you don't think it was an Old Boy, do you?' The man was crestfallen that the place of his youthful triumph had been laid waste by an Old Shedburian.

'I was being flippant.' Then it came to him; this was Sloman. How could he have forgotten so aptly named a boy, always at the back, always ungainly, usually out of step? With schoolboy twisted logic they had named him "Speedy". 'You're Sloman, aren't you?'

'That's it, Sloman II, until my cousin left. He was Head Boy.'

And Henry remembered that, too. The older Sloman had been an athlete, good at all sports, and a scholar. As Head Boy he had sheltered his ungainly young cousin, leaving others to take punishment when offences were committed. When the Head Boy left they got even; they bullied Sloman, it was unfair, but his protector had gone and the awkward child was easy prey. Henry remembered the day in the changing room, boys keeping cave at the door while the wet towels snapped at Sloman's bare backside. It was Henry's towel that had drawn blood.

'Tell you what, Haughty, the square may have gone but the old chestnut tree is still there.'

Henry looked blank, he wasn't listening to the man. All he could hear in his mind was the crack of a wet towel.

'You know the tree, by the yard, where we roller-skated?'

Henry nodded. Others in the carriage were listening and wanted to know about the chestnut tree.

'Those were the best conkers I ever saw, and they still are, look.' To Henry's consternation his contemporary reached for the pocket of his discarded coat and brought out a handful of shiny conkers. He laid them on the table in the first-class carriage for all to see. Heads looked up, admiring Sloman's bounty. 'You'd think kids would've got them, but there were dozens lying about. Pretty good, eh?'

'They seem fine.' Henry wished he had been sitting in another carriage, better still, had travelled on another train.

‘They’re a good size.’ This came from a man in a dark suit sitting across the gangway working on his laptop.

‘Yes, I think they are,’ agreed Sloman. ‘I should have some string somewhere.’

He went through his jacket pockets, pulling out pieces of paper, more than one grubby handkerchief, a few coins and finally, with a flourish, a tail of string, growing longer, as if spaghetti was unravelling from a plate. More rummaging and he produced a penknife with a spike. Encouraged by the man across the gangway, he selected one of the conkers and carefully worked the spike to make a hole in it, then a length of string was cut and worked through the conker until he could tie a knot in it and dangle the prize in front of Henry.

‘There you are, Haughty. Looks like a champion to me.’

‘I wouldn’t be much of a judge and for heaven’s sake stop calling me “Haughty”. My name is Henry.’ Sloman looked at him; he said nothing. He had already selected the next conker and wiping the spike of his knife against his sleeve he started to make the hole for the string to complete his second fighting conker.

‘This one’s for you,’ he said to the man in the dark suit with the laptop.

‘Can anyone join in?’ the voice came from a lady reading the *Financial Times* further down the carriage.

Sloman paused, then shrugged his shoulders. ‘I suppose girls can play.’

Soon all the conkers were strung, Sloman practised his stroke, swinging a mean conker against the leather cushion of the seating.

‘You go first,’ he paused before deliberately adding, “Haughty”. 'Three goes in turn, and then the next pair has a go and so on, until there’s a clear winner.’

‘What’s the prize for the winner?’ the man opposite asked. ‘How about a kitty?’

‘Good idea,’ agreed Sloman.

‘OK, a fiver each,’ the man in the dark suit suggested.

‘A fiver?’ Henry was appalled. ‘Ten pence, more like.’

‘Don’t be a skinflint, Haughty,’ the dark-suited man spoke, Sloman laughed, Henry seethed. Quickly a kitty with twenty-five quid was on the table and the conkers allocated between passengers. Henry added his fiver.

‘You go first, Haughty.’

Henry swung. ‘Ha! You missed; you never were much good at sport, were you Haughty?’

‘Rubbish, you do better, Speedy.’ The nickname slipped out in the heat of his exasperation.

The large man, sweat beading his brow, stuck his tongue out at the corner of his mouth.

Thwack!

Henry’s conker whirled like a windmill on its string; by good fortune it stayed in one piece. It was his turn again; he swung a mighty swipe at Sloman’s conker. He missed again.

On Sloman’s next turn Henry felt a searing pain in his knuckles and dropped his conker on the carriage floor with an anguished howl.

‘Haughty cheated,’ called out the man in the dark suit. ‘He moved his conker.’

'I did not move my bloody conker, and the name is Huntington,' he glared back, hurt in both hand and vanity. It was ridiculous to say he cheated. It was Sloman. He deliberately hit his hand.

'Not so keen on the wet towel now, Haughty?' There was a wholly satisfied look in Sloman's eyes.

The train ran into Paddington Station; the occupants of first-class carriage 'G' were absorbed in their challenge; Henry stood at the train door, a handkerchief wrapped around his aching knuckles. His conker was lost on the carriage floor, three more had been shattered. Sloman and the lady with the *Financial Times* were fighting the contest to the last swing.

'Not much of a player, your friend,' said the man in the dark suit.

'He never was,' Sloman agreed.

Henry got down from the carriage, the eyes of the players following him along the platform. He pushed to the head of the taxi queue and sank back into the anonymous surrounding of a black cab, his knuckles throbbing, a trace of blood coming through his makeshift bandage.

'If only they'd chainsawed that bloody chestnut tree.'

'What's that you said, guv?'

GENERATIONS

Duty Sister Carter looked out from the care home window. Two women struggled with a child refusing to get out of their car. The older woman usually visited alone, her father Mr Arnold was suffering, the prescribed drugs of no use against his unending prison camp nightmare. He would soon have to be transferred to high-dependency nursing accommodation.

They met at the front door.

'Your father is no better, Mrs Cooper; a long visit will exhaust him.' Sister Carter looked with apprehension at the toddler moaning and pulling away from parental grasp.

'We won't be long, Sister. Dad must see Alice; she is his only great-grandchild, she lives overseas. They've never met.'

The toddler's mother smiled with a shrug struggling to wipe chocolate from the child's red cheeks framed with a ring of blonde curls. The girl wriggled in her mother's grip, desperate to wipe her own face.

'I'll come with you to check on your father, then if you'd call into my office before you leave; I'd like a word.' Sister Carter turned to the younger woman. 'There are swings and a slide in the garden if visiting is too much for Alice.'

'She'll be asleep in moments; the time difference is getting to us.'

A dim light flickered in his opaque eyes, the sound of voices broke into the jungle turmoil playing day after day in his mind.

Was this how it was to end, sweating under the harsh tropical sun, the stench of decay clogging his streaming nose? The Japanese guards forcing him to hold the wooden block with his arms extended for hours without end? If it slipped from his wilting grasp, if his legs buckled he would be dead, killed by a single stroke from the guard wielding the katana sword, severing all arteries in his neck, his blood mingling with the jungle earth as cockatoos screeched their chilling chorus.

'Mum, we mustn't wake him.' The young woman stared at the rigid shape of her grandfather on the bed.

'We've brought Alice, Father; she's your great-granddaughter, she lives in America. I've told you about her.'

His bloodshot eyes flickered.

'Speak close and clear, he will hear you. I know you've come far to see him, but not too long, please. I'll be in my office.' Sister Carter straightened crumpled sheets, checked the drip feeding the cannula in his bandaged arm, checked the notes at the foot of the bed and left the room.

'Let your grandpa have a look at Alice, dear.'

'He can't see, Mum.'

'Put her on the bed, he'll want to touch her.'

The wooden weight eased, his arms relaxed. The harsh corners became soft on his hands. A halo of blonde curls crept into his blurred vision. Gentle breathing on his chest eased his elderly, rasping breath, catching the rhythm of the warm bundle. Breaths of milky infant air nursed his worn cheeks; he relaxed back into the pillows as small hands clung to his shoulders.

They dozed together, the distance of their decades bridged to bring peace to his mind.

No one spoke in the darkened room.

Sister Carter, anxious at the time the visitors were taking, returned to the room to find tranquillity. The toddler sleeping on her great-grandfather's chest, two souls at ease after troubled days, the child's mother dozing in her chair and Mrs Cooper, tears on her cheeks, sitting silent and upright not daring to move.

Sister Carter sat beside her patient's daughter listening to the gentle breathing in the room; as she watched she heard a rattle from the old man's chest. He slipped away, at peace after troubled years.

The three women gathered around, the granddaughter lifted her dozing child from her great-grandfather's bed, her silent tears witness to the old man's passing.

DAISY CHAIN

Raucous singing drowned out the band as the concert in the orchard closed; the songs cheered the men and next day's duties were a blur.

Trudging along in the column, Mickey daydreamed. Whatever her father had to say they had an understanding. He hadn't asked her formally, on his knees with a ring, but they were going to be married. Her father would shout and bluster; Mickey was man enough to stand up to a bully. She would be home now after her five-in-the-morning shift; heaven knows what could be put on their table to eat with her father coughing through the day in a cloud of smoke and her mother lost with the stillbirth of the last child. Four siblings to care for when she might be studying; she was always reading.

Mickey could read; adventure stories not her deep books. Daisy prattled away telling him the stories she read until he begged her to stop. Now he yearned to hear her sweet voice.

'Keep marching, lad.'

Mickey straightened up, burdened by his pack, his rifle at the slope boring in on his shoulder.

'No use regretting the cider now, lad.'

'It was wine the lad was tippling, Sarge.'

'We'll break soon, get a cup o'char inside you; clear your head.' Sergeant McWilliams marched tall; his Scots grandfather had walked from Caithness to Yorkshire to get work in the mills, the sergeant was proud of it. 'It'll be cooler when the sun goes down, you'll get a kip when we're in the line.'

'With this bloody barrage banging on, Sarge?'

Hendrie was an old hand with a wife and children back home, his eldest a good-looking boy already out of school and working as delivery boy in their corner shop. Hendrie knew how far he could go in his banter with the sergeant.

Coarse serge uniform itched against Mickey's legs; sweat ran down his vest and his drawers, his skin rubbed sore at his collar. Tea would refresh, the wine had been good, but there'd been too much, the old Frenchie kept refilling his mug.

Prayers and a hymn to follow before the last leg up to the line; the padre, a scholarly man confused by the circumstance of war, cut a weary figure, his dog collar sprouting from his uniform without any crisp white surplice to wear.

Mickey had sung in the church choir. He gave up going on Sundays when he'd started man's work at the mill, but he went on the choir outing to Whitekirk Abbey, walking with the drayman as the girls and women rode the wagon. That's when he'd kissed her, hidden away from the others within the roofless ruined nave of the abbey, and she had let him. Mickey yearned for Daisy's kisses, her moist lips and the tremble she made when they touched.

Her name wasn't Daisy, it was Helen, but he called her Daisy. She was always picking the bright flowers to make into chains. She'd put a daisy chain around his neck the day he'd kissed her. He'd pressed it flat between the pages of *King Solomon's Mines* which he kept on the shelf of his bedroom, the airless room he shared with his brother. The kid would be old enough for uniform by Christmas.

He'd promised Daisy he'd buy a bicycle, a two-seater and take her riding out in the country like in the song. She'd laughed, said he'd never save enough money, not for a tandem.

Mickey stood in line with red-faced men, the smell of sweet tea stirring his reverie. When his turn came the tepid brew – at the front of the line it had been too hot to drink - rich with sugar, soothed his throat as he gulped it down. Crossing to a turf bank he picked out the daisies amongst poppies and cornflowers growing through wilted grass. His fingers were awkward, he couldn't keep the flowers neat to make up a chain; he put the white petal flowers together in a posy and threaded it through a buttonhole on his tunic.

'What're you doing, lad? Giving sniper Fritz a target to aim at?'

'It's just a reminder, Sergeant.'

'His girl's called Daisy, Sarge.'

'Her name's Helen, honest.'

'Not when you call out in your sleep, it ain't.' Hendrie smiled; he meant no harm.

'Get fell in for the padre, lads. Look sharp now.'

Shivering isn't fear. Wrapped in his anti-gas cape against early morning chill, Mickey nursed his thoughts waiting with a line of men against the timber wall boards, his boots in water on the trench floor. The scream of artillery overhead cascading into no-man's-land and beyond.

'God help Jerry,' muttered Hendrie drawing on the pipe that seldom left his mouth, its rich aroma of sweet tobacco hanging on the morning air; Mickey wanted a pipe to smoke, folk respected a man with a pipe.

Rain had poured down until the last hot days of June dawned without a cloud in the sky. Duckboards floored the entry trench; the rest was mud, acres of mud blown into weird shapes and cavities by bombardments hammering down. Then there was the bloody wire.

On night patrol last time in the line they'd blundered about on uncertain footings in no-man's-land, hands and clothing caked in mud catching on wire without warning, spread-eagled when flares lit up the moonless sky. Four men and the platoon commander, Lieutenant Roberts, had gone out; Alfie was still out there, Mickey heard the crack as the bullet clanged into his tin hat and Alfie staggered back into the wire. They couldn't get him free; dawn was lightening the eastern horizon. Alfie hung bleeding on the wire through the morning held up between earth and sky. When the sun stood high overhead a shell exploded in the wire; nothing remained of Alfie for the next patrol to bring in.

Twice Lt. Roberts came to their positions talking to the men in his platoon. He was a decent sort, he listened to problems. Deputy Cashier in a bank before he volunteered, his uncle owned the Cready Mill - folk called it the Greedy Mill as life was harsh there - but Mr Roberts wasn't like that; he was a man to follow. Mickey, Hendrie, Sergeant McWilliams, they were all confident. The artillery barrage had blasted their objective for days, the crescendo of bombardment deafening. If they survived, the poor devils under it would be begging for surrender.

Positions were stood to in the trench after rum had been issued. The mine at Hawthorne Ridge echoed above the barrage, the guns fell silent, whistles blew and they took their turn up the ladder into the mud of the wired ground. On the further ridge beyond their objective the blasted village of Serre caught morning light no more than the length of three football fields distant across the devastated landscape. As practised over the farm fields of Yorkshire they walked forward holding weapons at the ready.

Striding at his measured pace, Sergeant McWilliams looked along their formation, unexpected machine gun fire strafed across their walking line, his mouth opened to shout orders to steady his men, but only blood and his life gushed out into the mud. They fell all round, Mickey walked on, hands shaking, his legs hollow. He could see the enemy trench, see men standing in strange helmets watching the carnage. He focused on the dugouts pointing his bayonet thinking of limp sack targets stuffed with straw that had swung from rails as they'd plodded over moorland turf with officers' whistles blowing in the sharp North Country frost.

A dull thud hit hard, he heard his knee shatter before pain seared up his spine. Mickey screamed and fell, rolling into a shell hole landing on a soft shape that stirred. Lieutenant Roberts lay with a leg severed from its thigh, his blood mixing with Somme soil, a grimace on his lips.

'I'm done for, Mickey.' The familiar face had grown old, his eyes could barely open. 'Take my field dressings, you'll make it, look after your wound. They'll get you back home…' His words were lost, foaming red, as he choked.

Mickey came to with sun beating down; he'd made what shelter he could from his pack and cape, the stink of cordite, mud and blood betraying the golden summer day. The pain in his numb leg throbbed; he'd staunched his wound as well as he could. Mr Roberts had gone rigid beside him as earth thrown up by the fall of enemy shells cascaded down peppering their refuge with stones and the detritus of the battlefield.

Crows flew over late in the afternoon; rats sniffed the air by the crater's edge. Squinting into the sun Mickey knew Daisy saw the same sun shining down on Yorkshire streets as she clumped back from the mill, her feet heavy from her day's labour. Soon he would be home, no longer fit for service with his smashed knee, and they would marry. Mickey wept for home, for Whitekirk Abbey's cool broken pillars, for Daisy's gentle lips and soft kisses, his tears dripping onto the posy threaded into his tunic. The summer day faded to dusk. Mickey pulled himself up; he had to find a way out of the shell hole. It was dark; she'd be reading a book from the lending library to tired youngsters giggling at her story under their blanket.

A hand of mercy reached down to pull him by his arm.

'Can you crawl?' the rasping voice called. 'Get back to the lines if you can, there's help for you there; they'll get you back to the Casualty Station.'

'And Blighty?'

'Get crawling, Private; look for white tapes they'll get you through the wire.' The man, or angel, he couldn't tell which, was gone to find another broken soul.

Mickey mustered his strength, his arms pulled and he kicked out with the good leg to find the tapes. He had to tell them about Mr Roberts, they couldn't leave him out there dead. He must get help; they would go back. They would bring in Mr Roberts. Just find the tapes, the shimmering path to safety.

Hands gripped, close faces stared, water dripped and smoke drifted on the air, the sweet aroma from Hendrie's pipe. Daisy was coming. He reached for her to link her arm down the aisle of smiling faces.

Bicycle wheels sang as Helen pedalled, riding into the rain away from the strange railway station where she'd reclaimed her bicycle from the guard's van. She was exhausted from the terrible journey. She didn't ask directions, she had to find him herself from the many times folded and refolded paper she'd been reading on her journey. She pedalled her bicycle past unfamiliar buildings, her child clinging to her waist astride the padded bracket.

When she walked between the neat rows the child hung back. A gardener looked up from his toil, watched the woman and child approach, took off his hat and rested on his rake.

She found Mickey's place. Her fingers traced the date chiselled into stone: '1st July 1916', lips moving as her fingers read. Helen trembled, kneeling on wet foreign grass sorting the flowers now limp from her journey far from home.

'Mickey, my only love, it's been so long. I wanted to come, dear, brave darling.' She reached for the girl to stand close. 'Mickey, this is Daisy, your girl Daisy. I wrote to tell you. The letter was returned, unopened.'

The child gazed at the line of graves flanking her unknown father, the stones standing in rows as straight as on a parade. She whispered the names she read: 'Lieutenant Roberts, Sergeant McWilliams and Private Hendrie. Look, Mum, it's the same name as Mrs Hendrie at the corner shop.'

AT 25 LUCKNOW TERRACE

Bright paint-washed houses vied with each other along the terraced street, their paved and planted front areas competing, their shining four-by-four vehicles lined up along the kerbs. South of the river, Lucknow Terrace had come up in the world. Young City professionals had moved in where more than a century ago upper middle-class Victorian men had lodged their mistresses a short Hansom cab journey from their solid City offices.

Since those days the terrace had languished through wars and decades of obscurity until its rediscovery by new City money at the turn of the Millennium.

The houses along Lucknow Terrace had been refurbished; all except number twenty-five.

Patches of plaster had fallen from its frontage revealing rough-bonded three-storey brickwork, painted window frames had peeled to rotting wood, the ground floor window had been broken and blocked from the weather with cardboard. Old privet and buddleia plants had grown tall against the house. For as long as any newcomer remembered, grubby curtains had been drawn across the windows. Number twenty-five let down the appearance of the street. It was discussed at local panel meetings, notes of community protest had been put through the letterbox.

Number twenty-five had not changed hands in seventy years. Its sole occupant was born there shortly after his parents had set up home following a long newly-wedded wartime separation. The occupant was seldom seen, only glimpsed as he sneaked out, running, to midnight shops.

Ernest tipped his breakfast bowl spooning up the last corn flakes, put the empty dish beside last night's unwashed supper plate on the wooden draining board, licked his spoon a final time before going into the dingy hallway, its dim light masking layers of dirt on a worn stairway carpet.

On the top landing he paused before a door, the air heavy with the clinging smell of oil paint squeezed from a multitude of wizened tubes. Piles of scribbled paper, empty boxes, wooden easels and broken frames accumulated over years waited inside.

A bare bulb hung from the ceiling adding to dull light from windows front and back masked with net curtains. Paintings, many yet to be finished, lined the walls. Ernest slumped into the only upholstered chair, his unkempt grey hair ringing his head like a lapsed halo.

A weapon was displayed, wired to the chimneybreast, a never-dusted wartime trophy from his dead father's Far East imprisonment. A kodachi honour sword, seized from Japanese hands, bearing witness to the Camp Commandant's suicide, kneeling in acceptance of his fate having failed in his duty to his Emperor. Ernest's father, forever locked in his nightmare, had shouted its awful history, aiming his resentment at his cowering son as he stumped up and down the stairway, waking the terrified boy. Even in his mature years, Ernest trembled at remembrance of his manic father's tread on the stair, dreading another beating for some misdemeanour known only to his persecutor's inner turmoil.

Ernest gazed at the sturdy easel in the middle of the room, its canvas hidden behind a paint-stained sheet. He wore a collarless shirt open at the neck, a torn pullover knitted by his mother in the years before his middle-aged belly bulged out over his belt and baggy cord trousers. He scratched his unshaven chin, a streak of cadmium red staining his cheek from paint his hand picked up on the door handle.

Some days he remained sedentary for hours contemplating the obscured canvas; on others he lifted up the cloth hiding the picture, but still left his brushes idle. On a few days he painted, peering at his work through thick-lensed glasses.

Ernest pulled back the cloth, examined the detail of the picture, stood back then started to paint, muttering as he worked, the more he concentrated the more he talked. Everything he did he explained to the painting, to the woman in the picture, her naked body sprawled in seduction across the canvas, lying back in the once smart upholstered chair.

He reached for a brush, poked its bristles into a twist of paint on his palette, pulling more paint into the mix until content with the colour, he took it to the painting. Time and place melted into the background as Ernest worked. No one had seen this picture except his late mother at its beginning as she had sat, fully clothed, for her portrait in old age. She would no longer recognise her portrait, nor the house she had scrubbed and dusted every day of her married life and widowhood.

A dozen years ago she had sat in the chair she and his father had bought the day after their post-war reunion, him too weak to lift the chair, their first furniture for the house; it had not been a new chair then, but a bargain discarded from a gentleman's house.

His mother had wanted to sit upright for her portrait; Ernest had told her to lie back in the depth of the chair. She would hate what had happened to her chair in the years since she had sat, dressed, for her son in the front room downstairs. The chair's stuffing had burst out from fabric ripped where Ernest had grasped the arms during long hours painting. In the picture the chair was still smart, as it had been in the front room, before he had lugged it up the narrow staircase, scraping against the walls.

'You're not cold, are you? I can feel the glow of your skin, you are warm enough.' Ernest worked with his brush, then took a palette knife from the jumbled table and scraped at the paint, flakes falling on the floor to be ground into the carpet as he shifted his feet. He took up his brush again deftly stroking paint onto the bared canvas.

'Don't move. You always move when I'm doing difficult bits,' he admonished his mute canvas. 'I must get this right. It hasn't looked good since you took off your clothes; I get your skin tone right, now your shoulder protrudes.'

Ernest stood back screwing up his eyes taking in his work.

'You've moved. I keep telling you not to move. You can be comfortable when it's finished. You don't need your clothes. The room is warm enough.'

Many layers of paint had been applied to the canvas over the years, sometimes painted over, at other times scraped down and built up again, as Ernest worked the portrait back through the years of his mother's life, back to the days of her youth when he was born.

When satisfied with her shoulder he only had to paint in the blue of her eyes to reach finality. Everything was there for the last touch to bring her to life, her long eyelashes familiar from childhood, the vacant whites of her eyes ready for him to unmask her, painting in each iris with the deep blue he'd known as a child.

'When you have eyes you will see me and see yourself of decades ago. You can look then, not before.' Ernest stood back; her shoulder was as it should be.

He gazed at the silky body full of passion, his creation, his ideal, the best, the only thing he had ever wanted to love in his life. Ernest knew there was nobody on Lucknow Terrace to match the woman of his childhood memory; none of the loud-voiced school-run women who had come to live along the terrace could rival his creation. Every sinew was his work, every tint and subtlety of her skin, the line of her limbs, the shy hint blossoming in gentle breasts, in the curve of her belly and the pleasure within her thighs.

Days passed and Ernest had not painted in her eyes; she was still trapped on his canvas. He paced his studio, hour after hour, trying to come to terms with the ending of his endeavour, to letting go, to admitting his work was finished; there could be no more days spent worrying for her. She was ready, he had to let her go, he had to start a new painting, a new private painting not one of the potboilers he took out at night to the gallery every few months to earn his income.

Late one night he reached for his brush, experimented as he had done so many times before on his palette forming roundels of blue until he saw the deep shade remembered from his childhood.

There was comfort sitting in his upholstered chair. An open bottle released its musk of red wine into the room, he drank a long draft, sat back and stared at the unseeing white eyes of the canvas until compelled to take up his blue-laden brush.

In the early morning hours, police tape was strung across both entries to Lucknow Terrace allowing only residents to pass. The fire crews were standing down, their task of saving the fabric of numbers twenty-six and twenty-four accomplished although both had suffered smoke damage. The top floor of number twenty-five was burnt out, its roof collapsed. The sole occupant had been taken from the building, found lying at the foot of the stairs, a Japanese war sword plunged into his belly.

In the ambulance the paramedic shook his head, the blood loss had been too great. He closed the victim's eyelids over fading blue eyes.

The garden gate swung back and forth in the breeze. The crowd of neighbouring onlookers was shepherded away by a duty police woman.

GOING OUT

Champagne flowed late into the night. Jane did without and slipped away as dawn broke and the others slept in the sumptuous hotel suite. The Saab convertible's comfortable purr eased her regrets, the keen morning air massaging her hair in the slipstream. Approaching Stonehenge she caught up slab-sided supermarket lorries slowing on the incline, the Saab responded, stretching its stride, to pass the wagons. The by-road junction would turn off in an another mile or two.

Would Great-Aunt Susan remember her? It had been two years since they last met.

My dearest Ian,

I should have written earlier. Now you've come here it's wonderful. These people see everything, they read my letters, search my cupboards; it isn't as if I'm a risk. I have top security clearance and you can vouch for that.

I saw you across the mess hall, tall, smartly dressed out of your uniform. I hadn't expected you to find me. I hate going into that mess hall. I eat my meals quickly and get back to my room.

You probably didn't see me, but I knew it was you sitting by the French window, the sun shining in and you not looking a day older. Are you still 'Lieutenant Commander'? It's been over for so many years. I heard you'd been knighted. Can that be true? 'Sir Ian', I like the sound of that: 'Sir Ian and Lady Latimer'... if only. Perhaps I made it up. The tablets do that to me.

I'm in Room 19. They permit visitors, but I don't get many. They allow me to go out if I'm accompanied, but at the front door I have to be signed out in a book, like a parcel. I try to get out without signing.

Remember the evening we sneaked out for a picnic high on the hills looking down on the sea loch, the depot ship fast on her moorings? We raced up the hill; you struggled, lugging our picnic basket.

Tall trees flickered sunlight into the lane as Jane eased the car, watching for the care home gates. Had she missed them before the by-road narrowed into this winding lane?

Tinned salmon and mayonnaise: we made sandwiches folded in slices of newly baked bread and we drank chilled champagne liberated from the wardroom, we had no glasses, we took turns to slurp it down from the bottle.

It fizzed over my face tingling down my neck; you unbuttoned my blouse to kiss it from my breasts until we shivered in the evening dew, a pale sun setting over Argyll's silent hills, standing guard over a gathered convoy.

The signboard was masked with clinging ivy. Jane used the width of the lane to turn in through iron gates the drive curving up a gentle hill until it swept in front of a white-stuccoed portico, too grand for the house standing behind it. Cars were parked nose-in to a wall. Jane sat flicking her hair into place, the electric car roof unfolding from its storage locker cutting out the sunlight. Eyes watched her from the house.

I wish I still lived in my home. I could walk around my own garden, sit in my old chair, sleep in my own bed for as long as I wanted, and most of all not take these bloody tablets.

Sorry, I shouldn't swear.

I hate the tablets.

I've missed you, Ian.

Your letters gave a hint of where your ship was bound; the censors never finding our hidden messages. Then no more letters.

Jane took a deep breath, pushed through the front door to the wood-panelled hallway greeted by a smell of disinfectant and furniture polish. A bell and a book for visitors rested on the counter. She pressed the bell and waited.

I'm expecting another trip soon; last time it was a troopship, sailing at speed, changing course to zigzag our way across. I was stuck in the signals shack, feeling sick for days decoding reports from the Admiralty about U-boats, passing their position fixes to nearby convoys, but the merchantmen were still picked off, blown apart as they wallowed on the bitter Atlantic swell.

It will be refugees and wounded outward bound for the United States, homeward a full ship of GIs, young boys who haven't a clue where they're going, but they're sweet; they look up to our deck blowing kisses and call me "Ma'am". New York is wonderful: shops full and no rationing. I'll bring back a suitcase of silk slips and nylons for the girls.

Last night a doctor came to my room; I hadn't sent for him. He said I wasn't taking my pills; they stand over me at pill time. I try to keep them under my tongue and spit them out when they've gone.

I almost forgot. Thank you for the carnations. Were they for my birthday? I didn't think you'd remember, not after so many years.

Thank you, my sweetheart; I am forever your Susie.

'I haven't been to a public house for a long time, dear.'

'Will you be alright under the sunshade, Aunt Susan?'

‘I’m indoors all day, dear. It’s fun to be outside in fresh air, away from the smells.’

‘Dad thought you might want to go shopping.’

‘There’s nothing to buy, everything is provided. Could you put my drink down for me? They didn’t give me a tablet this morning.’ The garden chair shook as the old lady gripped its arm. ‘How’s your mother?’

‘Fine, she’s lived in America since their separation. She must be enjoying herself or she’d be on the phone every day.’

‘I wondered why she hadn’t been to see me. Did she go with an American?’

‘Dad doesn’t know it, but she has a new partner.’ Jane felt at ease telling her great-aunt this gossip, a frisson of excitement in sharing the secret.

‘Partner, that’s what it’s called now. They were GI brides in my day.’

‘Did you have an American boyfriend, Aunt Susan?’

‘Not me, but I went to New York. Twice, on the *Queen Mary,* sailing as a troopship.’ The fragile old lady sat hunched under the sunshade, beaming at the memory, gazing out over the pub garden, her suit baggy on her now small frame. ‘Ian was my paramour, a young Scots naval officer. His ship was lost.’

‘That’s awful.’

‘It happened. It wasn’t an easy time to be in love: best just to be friends. Do you know what they said about the GIs and British girls’ knickers?’

Jane raised an eyebrow.

‘One yank and they’re off.’

'Aunt Susan.' There was a flickering smile on her great-aunt's lips, her watery eyes blinking. Was it her quip about the Americans or the memory of her Scots naval beau of so long ago? Jane reached across to hold the quivering hand, slack skin papery to her touch.

'Your top's too short, it doesn't tuck into your skirt.'

'It's the fashion Aunt Susan, cropped tops to show your hips.'

'You take after your grandmother even with your belly button on display. She and I had figures like yours when we were young, but navy issue undergarments were passion killers. Anyway, I'm your great-aunt.'

'Great-Aunt Susan, then; I've seen pictures of you in your WRNS' uniform. You looked gorgeous.'

'Undo my brooch, dear, it keeps coming loose.'

The waitress placed laden plates on the table.

'Is it too much for you?'

'It's real food, I'll eat the fish and a little piece of vegetable.'

'Will you have another glass of wine, dear?' The waitress hovered.

'I'm driving, but you have one, Great-Aunt.'

'Just call me Susie, dear. I've spilt most of this drink with this stupid hand.'

'And a slim-line tonic, please.'

The waitress smiled acknowledgement.

'I like your car, dear. Shall we put the top down this afternoon? Ian had a sports car, an MG, a 1933 J3, as I recall, he was so proud of it. We used to fly through the lanes when he could wangle the petrol.' There was a twinkle in the old woman's eye, a hint of colour on her cheek.

'I love my car, Susie. It's the best thing I ever bought.'

'You're doing well; your father told me you earn a lot of money in the City.'

It still hurt. For a moment Jane wanted to say yes, but why pretend to this frank old lady?

'I was made redundant, Susie. It's all over now.' Jane picked at an imagined hair on her lapel. 'I haven't told Dad; he always asks, every time there are cuts in the City. I tell him it's going well, but I haven't got a job, I haven't been in work for ten months.'

'You have a fine car, and smart clothes.'

'I'm living each day as it comes. It's the twenty-first century; a girl has to do whatever she can, with whatever she has, to earn money and… what the hell; I've got used to a life of plenty.' Why was she saying this to her great-aunt? Susie was bound to tell her father.

'Why is your father in America, dear?'

'He isn't. It's Mum who's gone to the States.'

'I saw Ian last night.'

'Ian?'

'He's come to take me away from that place.' For a while her hand didn't shake; Susie took up her wine glass, sipped from its edge, a gentle glow in her complexion, her pale eyes looking at Jane. 'You are right, dear; live as you can, but look after yourself, don't get hurt.' The glass shook as she took another sip. 'My excitements all happened long ago, then I missed my chance. I didn't realise it at the time, then it was too late.'

Jane watched swifts arcing across the sky, screaming as they swept over the weathered stone buildings. A column of midges spiralled in the sunlight.

'The fish was good; I can't eat any more, dear.'

Jane wanted to lean across and pick a crumb of fish off her great-aunt's blouse. 'Did you get the flowers, Susie? Dad sent them for your birthday.'

'I was surprised Ian remembered to send flowers after all the years.'

'You were not signed out, Miss…'

'Never mind that. I've had a good day out and I don't want you spoiling it. I have been out driving with Lieutenant Commander Sir Ian Latimer. He's a friend of mine. He will be calling again tomorrow.'

Jane lingered in the hallway; her great-aunt disappearing along the corridor, pursued by a care assistant.

'You'll need to find someone else for my room tomorrow; I'll not be coming back. Sir Ian will be taking me home.'

The car seat was hot from the afternoon sun. Jane unclasped the brooch Susie had given her, a gold navy crown picked out with small diamonds, a worn inscription on its back. Susie had laughed and waved as they'd driven with the roof down through summer villages, her thin white hair ruffling in the wind.

The hands-free mobile on the dashboard rang.

'Magenta, you left early this morning. You'll be back in time this evening, won't you?'

Jane sat in her car looking at the railings along the garden paths and the wheelchair ramp up to the front door. She traced the pattern of the warm brooch, sensing the little diamonds with her fingertip.

'Magenta, are you there? Don't let me down. You must get back; I've promised them you'll be here again tonight; they took a shine to you and it's a good payday for all of us.'

'Yes, Chloe, I'll be there. Give me a couple of hours.' Jane revved the engine putting on her dark glasses and a pair of calfskin gloves.

A RING FOR RITZI

I made a fuss at having to clear out her flat; why me? You get picked on when you're the youngest in the family and waiting to hear if your exam results are good enough for university; the others said they were too busy.

In truth I had nothing else to do. There were no valuables left in the flat, jewellery or the like. They'd been sorted out and taken home as soon as it happened. I discovered things hidden away, intriguing things in a nosy, forbidden sense; things that were private. She hadn't thrown them away, not burnt them or done anything final to destroy them. Perhaps she'd wanted them to be found.

Two boxes were hidden at the back of her airing cupboard on shelves stacked high with piles of old linen and worn-out towels. It's not as if she'd lost her marbles; my parents said she was exasperating, that meant she wasn't prepared to do what they suggested. She was as sane as any member of the family; maybe she'd wanted to tell us something.

There were photos in the boxes. She'd been in the war; she would talk about it if I asked her. She was in the air force, not a fighter pilot like women today flying jets. She was one of the people you see in black and white movies with a long stick pushing model planes over room-sized maps, plotting the state of play, as hostile bombers tracked in over south-east England. It was no surprise to find photos of people in uniform, but it was hard to work out which of the blurred grey shapes might be my grandmother amongst the distant groups posing fixedly for the camera.

It was weird being there on my own, in a nervous silence apart from the muffled radio from the upstairs flat. I'd half expected her to come home from shopping, to ask what I was doing sitting at her table, the contents of her two hidden boxes spread out in front of me. She hadn't been out shopping for months; we did it for her, calling in most days to see she was alright. She had an alarm call button to press if she needed help; she was meant to have it on a string around her neck. She usually left it by her bed. She wasn't an invalid or anything; she just had to sit down a lot.

'Who was Ritzi?' I asked them at supper.

'Haven't you seen the mangy draught excluder snoring by the fire?'

'Shut up, Henry. You know I promised Mother.'

'And to take on the vet's bills?'

'Don't be mean.'

They always bickered, and now it was usually about Ritzi. 'I don't mean the dog. Who was Ritzi, the person?'

'No idea, Andrew. Why do you ask?'

'Just wondered.'

You'd think he wouldn't begrudge the vet's bills; after all they are selling the flat, which must be worth a packet. They don't like dogs; Mum told me there were never any dogs when she was growing up. Granny got her first dog when my grandfather died and she was left on her own. All her dogs were called Ritzi, three of them over the years, all dachshunds; it's an odd name, even for a dog.

The photos set me thinking. Those people must have meant a lot to each other in the days before the war ended and they went their separate ways. She'd never talked about her companions, but one photo showed six people, four sitting in a jeep and two standing in the snow, on the back it said "New Year, 1943". The background was a flat open space, a few buildings in the distance and what looked like a windsock. Another photo had names on the back, but it wasn't possible to link the names to the faces, they'd been written at random, as if added years later.

"Catch, Walt, Splash, Maggie, Moose, Ritzi".

That's how I'd known there was someone called Ritzi, but which of them? Was it the one with pilot's wings on his uniform? They were older than me, about the same age as my sister. Strange to think of Granny as a young person; she was always old.

Why call every dog 'Ritzi'? She'd never had a dog called Splash or Walt, or Catch. You couldn't have a dog called Catch. It sounded daft. 'Here, catch, Catch!'

One of the boxes had typed and printed sheets in it. A dinner menu: 43rd. Sig FEM, Brussels, 23rd July 1945, with a list of names, formal names: LACW Bunting, P. was on the second table. There was a programme for a station entertainment, monologues, songs, recitals, each attributed to one of the company. Amongst the musicians Pamela Bunting played the piano. Even with arthritic hands my grandmother had played the piano, gentle melodies, accompanied by the knocking of the antiquated keys on her old upright. And there was a Ritzheim Westerhouse listed to recite the poem, "Daffodils". That must be Ritzi. Perhaps he was American, but why would an American choose Wordsworth? Was he aircrew, maybe the pilot in the picture? Who knows? Always more questions to ask than answers given.

There was a letter, no envelope with it, no date or sender's address, just the letter. Reading it again and again, I strayed into a place that was secret.

Dearest Splash,

The station is dull without you. I hope the new place is OK. Write soon. It was heaven at the cottage for our August week. We didn't know then you were going to be posted away, but we couldn't have chosen better if we had.

I'm so happy you're pleased with my painting of you, and that you'll let me keep it. I promise no one else will see it, just me when I'm feeling low.

Write soon, Darling. Ever your Ritzi.

In Granny's wobbly old-age hand with a blobbing Biro she'd written at the bottom of the letter.

I want Ritzi to have my diamond and ruby ring.

I had a mission: I had to find Ritzi.

There was still the chance to call it off; gold lettering at the base of the window declared the gallery's hours to be "10:30am to 4:30pm". It was a quarter past ten.

A stout wooden easel was positioned to look out onto Bond Street holding a garish oil painting. Other paintings were hung on the walls and at a desk, in the further reaches, a woman was working at a keyboard.

In the coffee bar across the street I ordered a latte and a cheese bagel. The seat in the window proved to be a perfect spot for watching the gallery. The woman unbolted the door at a studious five minutes after the half hour; no one visited before the postman called just before eleven, long after my bagel was eaten and I'd drunk the last of the cold latte.

The glazed door was shut; a voice came from a speaker. 'Can I help you?' The woman at her desk was looking over.

'Ritzheim Westerhouse: I think there was an exhibition of paintings here last year.' A man stood beside the far desk looking at the door over half-lens glasses, there was a buzz from the intercom, and the door unlatched.

It'd taken me only minutes with a search engine to find last year's Westerhouse Exhibition at Sable's Gallery; a full hour had passed since I'd arrived in Bond Street and plucked up courage to enter the gallery. A deep carpet deadened any sound in the white-painted space. The gallery smelt of polish, daylight filtered in through a roof light where the gallery extended back into the inner well of the building.

'And what, young man, is your interest in Westerhouse?'

'I have something to hand over. It's from a colleague who knew him years ago.'

The man, tall and superior, smiled dismissively. 'We can take it for you, if you wish, but Westerhouse is elderly and never answers the telephone. We have to wait for Westerhouse to contact us.'

'It's urgent. I'm charged with giving it to him in person.'

'I fear you have the wrong Westerhouse, young man. Miss Westerhouse is a very private individual; she doesn't welcome visitors whatever their business.'

Over my second coffee of the morning I told them all I knew of my grandmother's friend Ritzi. The ring, wrapped in tissue paper and checked in my pocket many times as I had journeyed into town, had been removed from the locked drawer of my father's desk. I'd found the place he hid his spare key months before on one of my prowls around his study. The woman held the ring to the light looking closely at the setting. She thought it to be Victorian, and of value. Together they examined the photos taking a magnifying glass from the desk. They pointed to the woman at the steering wheel of the jeep. 'She certainly has the look of a young Westerhouse.'

The taxi driver sat in his saloon car with his belly stuck behind the steering wheel looking at the directions written by the gallery on the back of a postcard of a painting from the Westerhouse Exhibition. A rush to Liverpool Street Station from the gallery - they'd summoned a cab on the gallery's account - a queue to get a ticket, a run to the platform and I'd caught the express that wound its way out of east London, past the grimy backs of houses presenting their better facades to the streets identifying their address. From Ipswich a single carriage branch line shuttle had got me to the truncated platform of a once much bigger station in Felixstowe.

The taxi, marked out from other saloon cars by the lopsided sign held on its roof with elastic straps, had dropped off a woman with a toddler and pushchair; the driver remaining rooted to his seat as his fare struggled to hold the child and unfold the awkward stroller.

After a while the taxi driver nodded and we drove out of town along diminishing roads winding into the countryside until the taxi weaved around deep potholes on a rough track to reach a cottage standing back from marshland. Beyond the white painted house mudflats went down to a tidal river.

Two birds, long beaked with a plaintive cry, flew by from the estuary on a salt breeze making for the farmland behind the cottage.

Dark clouds, full and purple, were piled high into the sky. There was a movement in a downstairs window.

'Miss Westerhouse?'

'The mower is in the shed, young man. There should be petrol in the can.'

I didn't question her greeting. Clouds threatened rain as I looked at the old rotor mower and the rough lawn grown tall. With a few pulls of the worn starter cord oily blue smoke billowed out, the rotor turned and cut into the overgrowth. The mowing, long overdue, left the ragged lawn strewn with chopped grass, but somehow looking neater for the cut.

With the mower stowed back in the dank hut the old lady reappeared asking if I wanted a drink. She wore what looked like a cricket sweater from generations ago, a faded vee of colours at the neck, its elbows worn through to strands of wool, she had on cord trousers with paint marks where her hands had wiped the fabric and a woollen hat which had seen better days.

'My name is Andrew; my grandmother was Pamela Bunting; I've brought you something she wanted you to have.' Why spin out my story? I'd learned not to do that at Sable's gallery in the morning.

'Splash?' She stood open-mouthed, her grey eyes blinking behind dirty spectacles, trying to focus. For a while she looked away in silence then stared at me again, wanting to make me out. 'Splash is your grandmother?'

'Why do you call her Splash?'

'And you live in the village? How is… you said she was your grandmother.'

'She died last month. She was eighty-two.'

'I'm eighty-five… poor old Splash… Pamela, but I never called her Pamela. Did she live near here?'

Ritzheim Westerhouse sat at her cluttered kitchen table, occupying the only chair. She held a key in her hand, an old-fashioned padlock key tied with string to a worn label. The key tap-tapped the table from her effort to hold her hand still.

Cold lemon juice poured from a jug covered with beaded cloth, against the flies, was welcome after my exertion with the mower. My shoes, damp from the lawn, had brought grass into the kitchen. The room, smelling of turps like the art room at school, was cluttered with unclean paintbrushes muddled with knives and forks, plates with scrapings of past meals and broken-handled mugs on the wooden draining board. She watched as I looked for a bin to discard the grass I'd brought into the house.

At the gallery I'd seen the catalogue of her exhibition, seen reproductions of her paintings. The exhibition had sold out in days. Here, in her cottage, pictures were propped on shelves and stacked in overlapping piles against the walls; her painted patterns of mudflats, filigrees of flotsam, broken boats, craggy fishermen and long coastal seascapes.

'My grandmother told me you painted a picture of her, when you were friends in the war. I would like to see her portrait as a young woman.'

'You've brought something from her?'

'Yes. It's a ring.'

'Poor Splash. I suppose she married him. That would be your grandfather, he was an awful drip; decorated in the war, but wet enough to wring out, and he was an unmitigated snob.'

'I didn't know him. He died soon after I was born.'

'She was a widow? I didn't realise; we had no contact after the debacle.' Her blinking eyes surveyed me, eyes of an artist seeking the essence of her subject before committing paint onto canvas. 'Splash took me home to meet her parents after our posting in Brussels, but it was a disaster. Her folks didn't care for me, nor I for them. Things were different in the days when she and I were young; there was no tolerance.'

Her fumbling fingers struggled with the tissue paper until the ring fell onto the kitchen table. Her head shook; she sniffed remembering excitements of long ago.

'I gave Splash this ring. It was my mother's engagement ring; she died when I was five; it was only me and my father after that, refugees in our adopted land.'

'Why "Splash"?'

'Your grandmother could swim beautifully, but she never got the hang of diving. It was a little cruel, but it was the spirit of the time.' The old lady gave me a long look, perhaps seeking some shade of the past in my looks.

'She had a dog. She called it "Ritzi".'

Miss Westerhouse laughed, lighting up her lined face. 'When I left her, after that awful weekend with her parents and the young man who was to be your grandfather, I told her I would get a dog, a little dog, and call it "Splash".' She pointed to a faded photograph on the wall. It was a dachshund.

'Andrew, I'll give you my painting of your grandmother. Look after it; it's personal, but I expect it's valuable these days. They wanted it for the London exhibition, but I'd promised her it was private. It's hidden in a frame on the stairs. Find the picture of a woodland cottage. Your grandmother's portrait is set in the frame on the reverse. Take it in exchange for the ring.'

A helmeted moped rider, a youth on his errand to mow the old woman's lawn, weaved past the puddles towards the cottage. I walked past him up the lane with the double-sided picture wrapped in brown paper under my arm, pondering how I could explain the missing diamond and ruby ring at home.

I could never show them Ritzi's painting of Splash; they would hate the picture, painted between lovers. It had to be my secret, my stunning, unexpected, secret.

Mission accomplished.

STING

I like the feel of soil on my hands, even wet dirt. You'd think mud would stink, but it doesn't, it's mushy, it dries on your hands then it itches and you wash it away till your hands feel good. Time spent outdoors is ace, better than being stuck inside. In a garden you can see birds, until a cat drops down from the wall and the bird is lunch. A garden is fresh, not lousy like sitting about indoors all day with crap telly.

I don't know why the old lady isn't around today. She's usually waiting when the van drops me off on a Wednesday afternoon, only there was no van today so I had to walk, aching head and all. It was miles up the hill out of town past the racecourse where I've had a punt or two in years gone by. The old lady has been ready with a pot of tea every time I've come here then she tells me what she wants done in the garden. There's no need for anyone to come to do the garden, it's neat as a pin; this is a cushy number, but why should I complain?

She had a go at me when I put sugar in my tea. I need at least four spoons even in her weak brew. First day I came round she couldn't find the sugar, gave me sweet tablet things; I tipped the lot down the sink. Sugar is in a bowl now, beside the teapot with the same flowery pattern and the matching jug for milk, never a box of milk. The sugar has a special spoon with it. I have to stir with a second spoon because the first one is part of the set with the bowl and she doesn't like me putting it back wet. I've never gone further indoors than the kitchen; I come around to the back door and she lets me in when I've wiped my boots. She is fussy about that.

Some days there's no outside work and she likes to talk, that's work in my book. She's lonely in a big house on her own with her husband dead. She talks to me since she found out I was in the army: her old man was a soldier. I told her I'd been in Hong Kong; she said she enjoyed her days in the Far East. I didn't, it was hot and sticky, and I spent time in the slammer after the rumpus in the bar. I didn't start the punch-up, but I got stuck in. The Yanks were in town off a ship spending dollars like there was no tomorrow. When the provosts arrived I was in the thick of it so I went on Company Orders and down to chokee. Twice I got promoted to corporal in my twelve years, Corporal Frankie Wilson then I got busted down again, so I was just Private Wilson when they chucked me out, no stripes, no wife, no kids, all gone. The wife legged it when I was in the glasshouse, took the kids and was gone, no idea where. The Staff Sergeant took delight in telling me she had done a runner when they let me out; he had a leer on his face.

'She's fucked off, Wilson, and the sooner you do the same, the better for all of us.'

Miserable bugger. Our Marlene will be leaving school this year, if she's been going to school, that is.

The old lady was impressed when I said I was in the Falklands and only eighteen. It was true, but it was after the fighting. It was the same with the Gulf the first time round. I don't let on that it was all over when I got there. I tried this lark of Gulf War Syndrome; they told me to get lost.

I cough a lot when I'm talking to the old lady; she says I should stop smoking. No chance, fags and booze is all the joy I get nowadays, too old for crumpet on the loose, even though they go around half naked showing rings in their belly buttons, even pregnant ones, tummies like basketballs sticking out from under T-shirts. I hope our Marlene doesn't go about with rings through her nose and who knows where else.

Anyway the old lady isn't here today. Odd that, no van, no old lady; I'll have to hang around and do my two hours; two hours a week for twenty weeks. They call it community service. Still, this is an easy pitch. There's nothing needs doing in the garden; you don't get paid or anything.

The shed isn't locked; I pull the mower out in case she comes back to check what I'm doing. There's an old lying-down metal deckchair in there, hottest day of the year the bloke on the radio said it would be, so I'll have a fag on the lying-down chair.

If I had a pen and paper I could draw something. I like drawing; I got a prize for it at school; it was a motorbike – not the prize, the drawing – everything accurate and I got it to shine like metal. Old Hicks, he was the art teacher, he said I should be a graphic artist, but you need exams and I didn't get to do any. I could draw people, real likenesses. I sold a few sexy drawings of birds with their kit off. I drew real faces, then bought magazines from filling stations and made the rest up, but with their bits bigger. Lots of the lads bought them, but that arsehole Widger left one lying about in the form room. The face was the Deputy Head and I got expelled. The Head sent me to apologise to her, said she was upset. I'm not sure she was; she looked at the picture before she threw it away and I swear she said, "if only". I bet she got it back from the basket when I'd gone.

I drew pin-ups for the lads in the barracks; blokes preferred them to magazine pictures, because I could make them as smutty as they wanted. I charged more for the porno ones; that got me into trouble again. You would think it wouldn't matter, not in the army.

I told the old lady I could draw people. She said I should draw a picture of her to send to her granddaughter in Australia. I didn't tell her why I was expelled from school.

Gordon Bennett it's hot. You can get cancer if you're sunburned, but I can take a tan, I'm not one of those milk-skinned gits who go red and peel flaky skin for days after. I go brown.

Thank heavens I've got a can of beer. Pity there's no paper, I'd like to draw something now, even a frigging flower and there are enough of those in the garden.

Shit, there's a wasp, a bloody enormous wasp buzzing inside the can; I felt the buzz on my lips. Double shit, there are two of them.

That's when I see it, up in the eave of the shed, this sort of fuzzy ball that looks as if it is made from brown paper, with wasps hanging around it. I must tell the old lady, damned if I'm going near it. Don't want her to be stung either; she must be in the house somewhere; she's always here on a Wednesday afternoon.

Rozzer down at the police station says the next-door neighbour saw me looking in the windows and rattling the back door; accuses me of trying to break into the house. Nosey bastard, what the hell did it have to do with him, twitching his upstairs nets? I've been going to the old lady for six weeks for heaven's sake.

I tell them I was there for community service. I'd hardly rattle the door if I'm trying to break in, would I? I've done six weeks at the garden, that's twelve sodding hours including today. I hate the nick; it smells of paint and disinfectant, late-night vomit and piss. It's always cold, even on a hot day like this and they treat you like a toad.

Says they'll check it out. I tell them the van takes me there, and then picks me up when I'm done. Only the van didn't turn up today, so I went on my own. I go every Wednesday.

The desk sergeant puts a *Daily Mirror* on the counter, pushes it over stabbing with his thumb at the top. It says "2nd June" - "*Thursday* 2nd June 2005".

Well how am I to know which bloody day it is? Every day is the same to me. I was on a bender, got drunk three nights running on the money I found. Well, it was in a wallet lying on the path. If some twerp is fool enough to lose his wallet, who am I to go waltzing down to the boys in blue with it? They'd say I nicked it. Like now, I do the decent thing trying to tell the old lady she's got a wasps' nest and they bang me up for attempted breaking and entering. Anyway, I got pissed out of my mind and I thought it was Wednesday today, only she wasn't there. She's always there on a Wednesday.

Sergeant says I was casing the place, it's my form, and it'll be more than community service this time. Says I did enough time locked up in the army to learn, and they should have sent me down, not let me off with gardening.

I told him I wanted to warn her about the wasps, didn't want the old girl stung; could be fatal at her age. He laughed, said I'd have to think of something better than wasps, put me back in the car to go and show them the nest.

Of course, there is no wasps' nest when we get back to the shed. It had been there, under the eave, I saw it with my own eyes, but nix, zilch, not a thing under the eave; collapse of alibi and the gloating constable puts his hand on my shoulder to march me back to the car.

'What's happening, Officer?'

‘Sorry, Ma’am. We’ve apprehended this man trying to break into your house.’

‘Nonsense, Officer, he’s my gardener.’

‘He gave us a cock and bull story, if you’ll pardon the expression, Ma’am, about a non-existent wasps’ nest.’

Bless her cotton socks; the lovely old lady just smiles at the fuzz. That’s right, Officer, she says, it was on the hut. She had to deal with it, went to the chemist to get the necessary, knocked it down with a stick then zapped it. Says if she’d known Mr Wilson - hear that, ‘Mr Wilson’ - was coming today I could have done it for her; asks the plod if he’d seen the dead wasps on the grass.

He just stands there silent with his mouth open; she asks if we want a cup of tea. With a bitter look at me he tails it back to the nick; I wipe my boots and have yesterday’s cake, and she asks if I’ve been ill.

On the kitchen table she’s got drawing paper and pens for me to make a start on her picture. She gives me a long look and asks if I’d been to a party and overslept on Wednesday morning. She’s a canny old lady this one, doesn’t miss a trick.

Then she stops me dead.

‘I’ve been in touch with the Salvation Army, Frankie; they’ve found out where your wife and children are living. They are well. It may be possible to arrange a meeting soon.’

THE PURPLE PATH

'Let me through… let me through, please.'

'Get back, there's a queue.'

'I'm staff. Let me through.'

'Stop pushing; what do you mean… staff?'

'I'm a minister of religion; I've been serving the Lord for fifty years, on his staff, so to speak.'

The Reverend Sandy Cornwallis was taken aback at the challenge to his calling. He looked at the crowd in front of him, a mass of people, so great a throng that he couldn't even see his destination. They were the sort of people he would call "riff-raff", though not to their faces, a huge crowd of people with the sweaty air of people needing a change of clothing. Come to think of it, he'd worn the same clothes himself for several days.

'Anyway, you haven't registered.' A tall balding man, his sparse uncut hair bound in a ponytail, prodded a stubby finger into the reverend's ribs.

'What do you mean… registered?' the minister fingered his dog collar, realising getting through was not going to be straightforward.

'You need one of these.' The man held out a plastic envelope strung around his neck with a card in it. 'It's a registration card.'

'I haven't been given one. No one said I needed one.'

‘You go to the pavilion over there.’ The man pointed back along the way Sandy Cornwallis had just journeyed.

‘That’s miles back.’ Sandy looked with consternation at the structure on the distant hill. ‘Can’t I just wait in this queue?’

There was murmuring all round. Everyone had registration cards slung on cords around their necks. ‘No way; they’re very strict. I queued for two days to get into the Registration Pavilion.’ The man looked at the minister with a hint of sympathy and the confidence of an old lag who knew the ropes.

‘Two days?’

‘Not as bad as this queue, mate; look for yourself.’

‘I can’t see how far it goes.’

‘No, look at the sign over there.’

Reverend Cornwallis looked at an electronic signboard about twenty yards further on. *Thank you for waiting: estimated queuing time 4 days.*

‘Oh God, this is ridiculous.’

His reckless call on The Almighty hushed the crowd, everyone stared. Sandy turned to trudge back along the way he had come.

‘No one said anything about this at Theological College,’ he muttered to himself, his feet aching from his journey of the last few days. *Life isn’t always fair*, thought Sandy Cornwallis, *neither is death it seems*. He’d spent his adult life working in the ministry and still he had to queue up with the herd of common people. ‘You would think they would have a “fast-track” system in place for people like me. Perhaps they do have a special channel. The registration cards were differing colours, red, buff and blue, maybe ministers of religion get another colour.’

He was puzzled, he hadn't seen anyone he knew or any famous person in the queue. He was left with the haunting thought he had missed his rightful path somewhere along the journey.

At last he was making progress in the registration queue, standing alongside an elegant lady. Out of politeness he raised his hat. She smiled with a coy bow of her head. Here was someone he could talk to, but for the moment he couldn't think of any topic to start the conversation. A self-conscious smile hovered on his lips before they both spoke at the same moment.

'I'm sorry,' he said. 'I interrupted you.'

'I was just going to say this is worse than Heathrow on an August Saturday.'

Sandy had never been to Heathrow on any Saturday, let alone one in August. He imagined it would be crowded and nodded his agreement.

'I expect the computer has gone down,' she added with a playful giggle. 'These systems never cater for peak loads. Still, we'll all get through in the end.'

As a man of the cloth it was not the reverend's habit for his gaze to linger on elegant women. He did think this lady attractive, she was sympathetic and she smiled a lot.

'Have you always been in the church?'

'Yes.' Pride in his vocation lifted his spirit, 'fifty years, and I'm a son of the Manse.'

'It was like that for me,' she said. 'I took over my mother's business.'

He was about to ask when the queue pressed forward and they had to jockey for position lest they lose their places.

The Registration Pavilion was massive, much larger inside than it appeared from the outside. In front of them they could see a long line of interview desks. Behind each of these there was a figure dressed in white. There were glass screens and microphones either side at each booth and a plain chair to seat the applicant. Another figure dressed in what seemed to be the standard white uniform stood on the yellow line at the head of the queue directing the waiting crowd in turn to their allotted places.

'Good day, thank you for waiting, stand number 791, please.' With a smile Sandy's companion moved off to the designated window.

'Good day, thank you for waiting, stand number 792, please.' Sandy Cornwallis followed quickly after her. For a moment he paused as the interviewer on stand 792 finished her paperwork. He took advantage of the small chair in front of the desk. He hadn't sat down since the start of his journey, even this unpromising seat looked inviting.

'Good day Mr Cornwallis, how are we today?'

'Ah, you know my name, I'm expected then.' Sandy's spirits revived at the chance he would be put into the fast lane.

'Yes, we make it our business to know who is coming through, but there is a whole lot more we need to know about you to get things underway. You speak English and you can read I take it?'

'Certainly; I'm a minister of religion.'

'Ah, that's nice. I need to get some more details, nothing too difficult.' The interviewer surveyed a form printed with boxes to be filled in. 'This won't take long.' The clerk wrote CORNWALLIS boldly at the top of the form with an "M" in the gender box.

'Forenames?'

'Alexander Maitland.'

'Date of birth?'

'May seventeenth, nineteen twenty-nine.'

'Eighty, that's not too bad, so sad when someone young comes through. Profession?'

'I told you, a Clerk in Holy Orders. Now I assume there is a special clearance for me in view of my calling.'

'Not really, dear. Everyone goes through the same system these days. We used to be able to pick and choose, sheep from goats, that sort of thing. Not now, everything has to be done on quotas, you know how they work, by age, by gender, profession, ethnic origin. Come to think of it we've had a lot of vicars, priests and the like through recently and a few bishops, so the quota could be quite full. Might be worth trying something else. Have you ever been a teacher?'

Sandy stared wide-eyed as the clerk chatted on working down through the form.

'Anyway, think about it. Some of the bishops were black so they have their own quota, as do the lady vicars. I've got your age and gender. Put you down for Caucasian, shall I? Now you don't have to answer all the questions, but I'll explain them to you, then parts two and three you fill out yourself, over at the tables.' The clerk pointed further down the large hall.

Sandy Cornwallis didn't catch all he was told. The news of quotas was disturbing. He'd taught in Sunday school. Would that count as being a teacher? As his mind searched his past, he found he was listening to the interview in the booth 791 with the attractive woman from the queue. He gathered her name was Janet and she was in her early sixties.

'And your profession?'

Janet leant forward and spoke very quietly into the microphone.

'That's no problem, dear. Everyone is equal in our books and all professions have their own quotas. P, R, O, S, pros, T, I, or is it two tees? I can never remember.'

The Reverend Cornwallis blushed and stared straight ahead his ears burning.

'Were you paying attention, Mr Cornwallis? Part two is where you list all the good things you've done in your life and part three is for all your sins. Now you must be honest, don't try to hide anything, good or bad, and do use black ink or Biro as we have to get the forms photocopied.'

Sandy was in a daze making his way to the table to fill in parts two and three of his form. There were chairs at opposite ends of each table and a dividing wooden piece, which made him think of the ping-pong tables in the youth hut. Janet joined him.

'Can I sit here, Reverend? All very friendly isn't it. Not a bit like the social security.'

It was plain to Reverend Cornwallis that Janet had been encouraged by her interview, while his mind was in turmoil. What was the point of being in Holy Orders for fifty years if there was no advantage at a time like this? He smiled weakly and attempted to rise from his seat.

'Oh, don't get up Reverend, if your feet are aching like mine a good sit down is what you need. Now I've got to think seriously about this form. It must be easy for you in your line of work; I have a bit of a past to get sorted out.

If only it was easy. Sandy looked at the blank sheet and wondered what he should write down. Would it be better to start with part two, the good things or should he start with his sins? Did they want every sin or just the bigger ones? He remembered the time he travelled on the train without a ticket, but decided they didn't mean things like that. Nonetheless he wished he hadn't remembered it. Perhaps he should try part two first. He took a pen from the jam jar on the table and held it over the paper.

Sermons: he enjoyed sermons and surely they had done some good over the years? Let's see, fifty years, say fifty sermons a year; mental arithmetic had never been Sandy's strong suit.

'Five fives are twenty-five,' he mumbled, 'add the nought. Is that two hundred and fifty?' He paused a while then realised it was much more than that. 'My word,' he liked the pun, 'two thousand five hundred, who would have thought it was so many?' He started to fill in his form, writing in a large script so that it took up plenty of the page before he noticed the small print at the bottom of the sheet suggesting a continuation sheet if more space was needed. His mind went blank. Janet was scribbling away with the tip of her tongue pressed out of the corner of her lips in an innocent, yet provocative way. He looked back at his own form.

He had taken the Youth Group to summer camp every year for at least twenty-five years. He could put that down as something good he had done, but even as he wrote he remembered the night of the storm when Mrs Burdock had been so frightened of the thunder, and her sleeping bag got wet, and he had to comfort her, and it was very dark in the tent, and… well, they never spoke of it again, but it had been very snug hugging each other in his sleeping bag. Mrs B was quite a woman under her ill-fitting uniform. Oh dear, he would have to make a start on part three, even if Mrs Burdock had been many years ago.

‘Excuse me.’ Janet was holding up her hand trying to attract attention from one of the assistants dressed all in white wandering around the tent.

‘Good day, Madam, how can I help you?’

‘Where do I get the continuation sheets?’

‘Do you want only one?’

‘I think I need one for both the sections, there seems to be so much to say.’ She smiled sweetly at Sandy with a knowing look.

‘Oh, hello Reverend, how nice to see you; I didn’t know you were coming through.’

The Reverend Cornwallis looked at the figure in white. ‘It’s young Tommy, isn’t it?’

‘That’s right Mr Cornwallis. I am pleased to see you.’

‘And you.’ Tommy had been quite a lad, always in some sort of trouble. ‘I see you’re an assistant here.’

‘I hope to be soon. I’m on probation at the moment.’

‘You always were, if I remember right.’ The words just slipped out before he could think what he was saying.

‘Oh, that’s good, Reverend. You always were such a laugh.’ He turned to Janet. ‘He was such a card, always making people laugh, he was.’

‘He kept me company in the queue, very much a gentleman.’ Janet looked across, ‘I wish I had known more gentlemen like him. Have you been here long, Tommy?’

‘It’s a while now.’

‘This probation,’ asked Janet, ‘do we all have to do that?’

'No, only if you want to get on the reception team. I've passed my provisional, next is intermediate, then if that goes well there are the finals.'

'Otherwise what do people do?' asked Janet.

'We all have to do the provisional, that clears the slate from any little problems you may have come in with, but you can just settle for that and relax; I was keen to press on. I think I should be ready for my intermediate soon, I've got quite an itch between my shoulder blades and I think there are some lumps coming.'

'What do you mean, Tommy? Not wings?'

'Oh yes, you can't get to finals without wings. You should see some of them, gorgeous they are, great sweeping wings, but they've been years in the growing.'

'Would you let me feel, the lumps that is.' Janet had dreamed about the angels when she was a little girl. They were so exciting.

'I shouldn't really, but seeing as you're the reverend's friend, it'll be alright.'

Tommy leaned over, turning his back to Janet and she gently stroked between his shoulders.

'Yes, there are definitely some lumps there. They're quite warm,' she added.

'I'm very excited, but the lumps can go away as easy as they come, if you aren't careful.'

'But I haven't seen anyone with wings here,' said Janet looking around the huge hall.

'No, you'll see them later. Still I mustn't chat all day. You wanted some continuation sheets.' He handed two sheets to Janet. 'What about you, Reverend?'

'I don't think I'll need more. Truth is I'm having a bit of difficulty filling up the page for part two.'

'Oh, dear me no, there's plenty you can put down. Remember when little Polly floated out to sea on the lilo and you swam out and saved her, then there was Mrs Burdock who got hysterics in the thunderstorm and you calmed her down, then they all said you would never raise the money for the church roof, but you did. I'd better leave you a sheet anyway.'

'Thank you, Tommy, perhaps two sheets.'

'That's it Mr Cornwallis, clear the whole slate at once. That's what I say.'

Janet was already on her second sheets and for a while the two of them wrote busily at their table without talking. Tommy went over to another applicant struggling with the form and spoke to him for a while before he came back to see how they were getting on.

'Just about done are we?'

'I feel better for getting all that written down,' said Janet. 'Where do we go next?'

'You get your registration cards at the far end; I might be able to help you along a bit. I'm very junior, but I am allowed to initial your forms. I'll take you both over to the special desk. We should be able to get you a timed entry at The Gates which will get you there without the long wait.'

'Tommy, that is good of you. I'm so glad we met again.'

'It's my pleasure, Reverend. It's true I was a bit of a tearaway in the old days, you were good to us lads and I know you helped my mum out after the motorbike accident.'

Janet gazed at the Reverend Alexander Cornwallis with a look that struck great contentment into his being. They followed Tommy to the registration desk.

'Two together here,' said Tommy, 'for a timed entry.'

The clerk looked quickly through the forms to see that they were completed and signed. 'That all looks fine. Here are your registration cards.'

He handed them both purple cards with the words *IMMEDIATE ENTRY* written on the top. 'Follow the purple markers and they'll lead you straight to The Gates.'

'It's best if you go forward as a couple at The Gates,' said Tommy. 'They prefer happy couples; it cuts down on all the arguments.'

'Perhaps you should read what I've written on my form first,' Janet looked with concern at Reverend Cornwallis.

'Oh no, I don't need to do that, Janet.'

'I'll let you get on your way, then. My shift isn't over yet; I'll look out for you.' Tommy watched Janet and Sandy as they walked off arm in arm along the way-marked purple path.

'What a pleasant couple,' said the clerk behind the desk. 'Such a contrast, I've had nothing but bother on this shift; complaint after complaint.'

A CORSAIR CALLS

'Reverend, Reverend, come quick, she's been taken.'

The calm in his study was broken, his concentration was lost; the pleading woman stood at the door panting from her running.

'Rebecca, collect your thoughts; who has been taken, and by whom?'

'The Barbary Pirates, Reverend, they've got Tall Susan, snatched her off the beach, they have.'

'Calm yourself, Rebecca.'

'She was collecting seaweed, they crept up and took her, rowed her out to their vessel and they're standing off a distance.'

'Are they setting sail?'

'No, Reverend Huxley, they're waiting. Tall Susan's dog got a pirate boy by the leg and pulled him into the water. Now our men will hang the boy from the market tree. You've got to come Reverend.'

Huxley paused, a prayer hung on his lips, his eyes closed; he took up his hat and strode down to the bay, Rebecca running on ahead. The Corsair was waiting, bold as brass with sails aback, a cable's distance off the shore. The fishermen had the boy, arms roped to his side. Old Matthew was pulling a rope over the market tree bough.

'Hold hard, Matthew, do not harm that boy or you'll answer to the Bridport magistrate.'

The village fishermen moved away. Huxley looked at the boy, sullen beauty masking the terror in his eyes.

'Jack, row me out to the pirate ship. Have no worry, Matthew. I will get your granddaughter back. Ephraim, you and Gabriel put the captive boy in your boat and wait until my parley is done, don't row out until you see Tall Susan on deck.'

Jack pulled hard toward the Barbary vessel, Reverend Huxley stood erect with his feet braced athwartships, keeping a standing balance, despite the chop of the sea. Aboard the pirate vessel men lined the rail with cocked pistols. The reverend stood firm, rehearsing the French he'd learned at school. Cupping his hands together he shouted over. 'Appelez votre Capitaine.'

The men at the ship's rail exchanged glances. The chief among them nodded to one of their number who went below to fetch the master.

A huge man came up on deck, the Barbary seamen easing aside.

The captain stared at Huxley. Jack's hands gripped the oars ready to pull for the shore, the minister held the captain's gaze, a seagull screamed.

Huxley called over, 'Monsieur Le Capitaine, je tiens à vous parler. Au nom de votre Prophète, paix soit sur lui. S'il vous relachez votre prisionnier, puis nous reviendrons a vous le jeune homme que nous avons fait prisionnier.'

The pirate captain glowered at Huxley. The reverend waited hearing the rattle of the ratlines, the idle feathering of the black sails holding the vessel steady against the incoming tide. The pirate master barked an order to his men.

Tall Susan, blindfolded, with her hands tied, was brought on deck. Huxley waved to the shore summoning Ephraim to row the boy out from the beach.

No words were spoken as Ephraim pulled alongside the pirate vessel. The sailors reached the woman down into the row boat as Gabriel handed the boy up to the ship's rail. The captain cuffed his ear and the boy was led below.

Ephraim pushed off from the ship's side and pulled hard to the shore.

The minister and the captain held their mutual gaze until, with a nodded salute, they acknowledged each other.

The Corsair's sails were set and she eased away from the coast.

LET IT BE ANTHEA

She goes ahead to find my reserved seat, makes sure I settle and can see my suitcase stowed at the end of the carriage, checks I have my magazine and picnic box, telling me to wait a couple of hours before eating my sandwiches on the long journey. After goodbyes she is off the train with only moments to spare before we are moving out of Leeds Station on the 07:05, cross country, bound for Plymouth.

Morag mothers me. It's not as if I've never caught a train before. I guess it's what daughters do when their fathers grow old and live on their own. Not like my twice divorced boy, Alec, now a professor at the Peninsular University, who can't meet my train as he's in a conference all day. My instructions are to take a taxi to his house where the door key is under a brick beside the front step and I'm to let myself in. He will be home late afternoon.

I don't think Morag knows this is a 'quiet' carriage. My new phone is complicated not like the old one which was a telephone and nothing else. I was given it on my birthday so I have to make the best of it. As I fiddle to turn it off, the flash goes and a photo of my tray table appears briefly on its little screen. The rocking of the train makes it hard to read, I watch the landscape slip by, at first the industrial towns of South Yorkshire and later farmland, some fields already cut for harvest.

I'm woken from my dozing by a knock against my seat as a snacks trolley works along the carriage. Cans of beer are stacked on the trolley.

We haven't got to Birmingham yet and I've eaten my sandwiches. I buy a beer, better than the carton of apple juice Morag put in my picnic box.

You'd think people would leave the washroom in the state they'd like to find it. The one in my carriage is unusable and we've only been going three hours. The one in the next carriage is little better.

I'm looking forward to travelling across Somerset to see if I recognise places from my youth, those years, "Far away and long ago", as someone said in a book I read in my days as a cub reporter on the County Gazette. Then I went off to national service, the army in Germany, later pounding countless streets as an ever more experienced, if not always appreciated, reporter on regional papers, a married man with growing children.

Bristol, wet and grimy, gives a glimpse of Brunel's suspension bridge. I once had to cover a suicide off that bridge, a young chap, he chose high tide surviving the fall into the water, severely shocked, only to die in hospital from hyperthermia hours later. They never found his next of kin, nor any note of why he did it.

The train gathers speed across farmland dotted with grazing cows over the flat lands of The Levels. Before I realise where I am, we pull into the familiar scene of the station with the longest platforms in the once proud Great Western Railway empire, platforms I knew well in the days I stood in short trousers by hissing steam giants, hot and oiled, after their haul from Paddington. With the others, I was never alone, always hoped to get an invitation onto the footplate, the name and number of the engine already written down in our spiral-bound notebooks. My book is to this day in a box above my bedroom wardrobe. I never mention it to anyone.

Nothing happens after the hubbub of arrival and intending departure settles down. The guard, I still call them guards, comes on the tannoy announcing a delay due to a rostering problem. After a few minutes he comes through the carriage and tells us a relief driver is on his way on an incoming train, but won't be with us for quarter of an hour. Across the platform from my carriage is a sign – *Gentlemen*. He agrees I have plenty of time and to take a stroll along the platform, welcome after four hours sitting in the same confined seat.

My wandering takes me through the booking hall, remembered but modernised, no longer Victorian hardwood carving, now glass and electronic screens, and out into the station forecourt. Across the road the Gaiety Cinema, the home of countless Saturday morning adventures, is now a billiard hall. The 'heavy' on the door says I can only enter if I'm going to play. The Duty Supervisor is more amenable and I get to look inside and chat about the days of Roy Rogers and Trigger on the black and white screen. Nothing of the old cinema's elaborate decor is recognisable.

Back at the station the downline platform is empty, the train and my suitcase are travelling on to Plymouth, the driver turning up quicker than expected and I dallied too long chatting by the pool tables.

Nothing is lost once I get my details – Mr James Crosswell, Coach A, Seat 51B and luggage description - sent down the line to Plymouth. I'm told to contact the Duty Manager when I arrive and the times of the following trains, one every hour. As I have to make my own way to Alec's house an afternoon looking around old haunts here rather than twiddling my thumbs waiting for his conference to finish, is welcome.

The shops have changed along North Street, gone is Mrs Palmer with her shelves laid out with fresh vegetables, also the Novelty Joke Shop is no longer. A favourite with kids without pocket money to the fury of Mr Norris, the shop is a kebab house. The butcher's shop is unchanged. I can only guess how many tons of beef have passed over those scrubbed marble slabs in the intervening years.

Further into town, once petrol-fumed streets are pedestrian spaces, interrupted by the bleeping tones of backing delivery vans. Too many town centre shops have whitewashed their windows or display closing down sales signs for there to be any real buzz about the place. And it starts to rain.

Judging by the sleet against the windows and the people rushing in shedding soaked coats, I've been lucky to have avoided the storm, get a table and my order in for coffee and a pastry. The second chair from my table is taken to make up a four at another table leaving me on my own to watch the waitresses coping with the unexpected rush. The building has gone through transformations from its Victorian beginnings, once a meeting hall, then an auction house, now a café serving meals to lunchtime office staff and shoppers. A large space extends from the tables to the street doors showing original polished floorboards dampened by the rush of folk coming in from the storm.

The teenage years I spent in this hall surge into my mind. Mother insisted I went to dancing lessons in this place, always hanging back, standing against the wall with rain-soaked trousers from bicycling to my lessons, until Miss Mountjoy called me out to introduce myself to one of her girl pupils; it was always a taller girl. Yet I was good at the foxtrot, responding to the rhythm without too many foot faults.

'Let it be Anthea,' I whispered to myself every time Miss Mountjoy's all-seeing eyes cast around the hall pairing up her pupils. Anthea was my age, well three weeks older to be precise – I'd glimpsed the register one evening and kept repeating her birth date all the way home determined to send her a card when the day came.

Her parents brought and collected her by car every class, never any damp clothes for Anthea. During the second winter of our classes we were sometimes picked out to demonstrate a dance to the class, responding to Miss Mountjoy's running commentary, but in all that time we hardly spoke. She didn't return for the third winter, I only joined in the hope of seeing her. And she never acknowledged the birthday card I slipped through the letterbox of her parents' detached house on the well-off side of town, bicycling away in the dark, hoping not to be seen.

A queue has formed, hopeful customers looking for seats. I sit tight, the rain still heavy and I'm in no hurry with regular trains, to finish my journey.

Across the room a woman, much my age, sits staring across the tables, a man and a woman, probably a married son or daughter, sit either side of her trying to get her to engage and eat the cake on her plate.

It cannot be; I walk across to her table.

'Anthea?'

She doesn't react. Concern on their faces, the man and woman look up at me.

'Anthea, it is you, isn't it?' I know she hears me. Sixty years may have passed yet as she turns lifting her head her eyes are the same eyes I could never look into without blushing.

'James, is it our turn again?'

The rhythm is in my mind, and we share it. She stands rising from her chair with difficulty.

The man at her table is uncertain. 'Mother, are you alright?'

'James has asked me to dance, Michael. He's such a polite boy.'

No longer are her eyes above mine. As if our classes were yesterday, we take each other in a formal hold, and slowly move into the room as the queuing customers ease back to clear the floor.

We don't speak. Minutes pass as our floor space grows with customers pressing against the walls enjoying our dance. The man and woman at her table watch in amazement as we circle round at our slow foxtrot pace.

They stand and applaud, tears running down her son's cheeks, as I guide Anthea back to her table, our dance done.

'I enjoyed your birthday card, James. It was thoughtful of you. Come on Michael there's no call for tears when your mother goes dancing.' Seated she turns away back in her staring state.

Michael drives me to the station. We are greeted on the platform by a manager newly on shift.

'Everyone is looking for you, Mr Crosswell. There's a proper fuss going on. Your son went to meet you at Plymouth and you weren't on the train. He and your daughter in Leeds have been trying to ring you. Your phone is turned off. Any longer and we would have got the police involved for a missing person's enquiry.'

'But my son said he couldn't meet me, he's at a conference.'

'He was at the station to meet you. Next departure for Plymouth is in five minutes. And you better be on it and turn your phone on. You'll find there are messages waiting.'

Michael looks on. 'I'm sorry about the fuss, Mr Crosswell.'

'It'll blow over. I did enjoy meeting your mother again. I hope I haven't upset her.'

'Not at all, the tonic you've given her today has been wonderful. Who'd have thought it, sixty years gone by and she knew you as if it were yesterday. There are days she doesn't even know who I am.'

Michael blinks wet eyes. ‘I didn’t know she could dance like that. It’s the best day she’s had in years.’

We shake hands and I search for my phone.

HENRY'S HEN NIGHT

On a warm evening Henry walks into town as high straggling clouds reflect crimson strands from the late-day sun. There is little prospect of rain, but he carries a tightly rolled umbrella. A vivid pink stretched limousine with darkened windows passes by along the far carriageway.

Henry has a particular destination in mind for the evening. It involves a wide television screen, a convivial atmosphere and a cricket match taking place on the other side of the world. He intends to watch the opening hour, or so, while he enjoys a pint of real ale from a local brewery. Then, having seen how the cricket is setting up, he'll return to his apartment to listen to the Test Match Special broadcast through the night.

Such an evening would not have been possible in recent years, his hours taken up, day and night, with family caring duties. With those years in the past, he misses his parents, his mother most of all and the hours he spent with her. It was a remorseless routine, yet now he finds it hard to fill the days.

The family house is sold, not a grand house, but a worthy home reflecting his parents' dedication to hard work. His new place is an apartment with modern facilities, too small to be considered a flat, but much more than a bed-sitting-room, one of seven in a converted Victorian villa. Unicorn Apartments is a fine building on the edge of the town with a gravelled drive curving through neat gardens. Henry had a choice and opted for the ground floor apartment. The stairs, while not challenging today, might well become a problem in the years ahead. The other, and larger, ground floor accommodation is the home of his landlords, Mr and Mrs Patel. Henry has known the Patels over many years as owners of the local pharmacy.

He'd hesitated over what, if any, of his household belongings to bring to his new apartment. With no younger generation to consider, he got rid of things. He wanted a fresh start on his own, but he'd decided to keep the silver cup he won years ago - not many people win a trophy in Blackpool's Tower Ballroom.

The pink stretched limousine passes by again, driving circuits around the town, its occupants celebrating, a window open and a girl holding out a glass, calling to the crowd along the street.

Ahead, in his path, a canvas canopy bridges across the pavement, decorated with bunting and balloons. People mill along the pavement and pause, wondering what celebration is afoot.

The pink limo completes another town circuit gliding to a halt by the awning over the pavement. Two chauffeurs step out to open the double side door of the limousine, and one by one a bevy of eight girls steps out, pulling down scrunched-up hemlines over long legs, strutting across the pavement on high heels under the awning, their shrill voices calling out in party spirit. They make their way to the nightclub entrance.

A blonde and perfumed girl, in a tight black dress, stumbles off her high heels, saving herself from falling as she grabs Henry's arm. The blonde girl stares at Henry as her eyes well with pain. 'Bloody hell, I've done my ankle.'

'Lean on me a moment.'

And she does, as her seven companions strut in through the nightclub doors.

'I'm always ready to help a young lady. Can you walk on your ankle?' And without more ado, with slow steps, Henry escorts the limping youngster across the pavement.

Her friend looks back. 'Who've you got there, then, Kaylee?'

Another girl, standing beside the door keeper, calls over. 'Hello, Grandad, you coming to the party, and all?'

Instead of sitting in his anticipated armchair watching the cricket, Henry walks inside to the loud inner depths of throbbing rhythms in the nightclub's inner sanctum, the girl, Kaylee, hopping beside him, clutching his arm.

'You must get that ankle looked at in case you have damage,' suggests Henry.

'And miss the party, no way, I'll rest it a while.' Kaylee holds tight to his arm.

The eight girls gather round a decorated table to celebrate Amy's soon-to-be wedding, her name spelt out on a multitude of balloons, tied to the chair backs.

Henry protests he must be on his way, but a waiter is summoned and ordered to set another place, and 'Grandad Henry' is given a seat of honour between Amy, on her night of delight, and Kaylee, still holding his arm.

Instead of a pint of real ale, Henry holds a glass of bubbly with the admonition he is already two rounds behind the girls and must catch them up. The girls lift their glasses and chorus 'Welcome, Grandad Henry!' whooping their enjoyment.

A tall girl, Debbie, is the shy one, and the one with her hair dyed pink is Mel, but says it isn't her real name. She's got a place at university a year ahead, but doubts she'll have the money for it. Amy, whose hen night it is, tells Henry she has a little boy, two years old, her husband-to-be isn't the boy's father, but he loves them both. The others on the far side of the table are too far away to talk to over the noise in the club.

Kaylee rests her leg on a spare chair Henry has brought over for her, her prawn cocktail starter untouched. She insists on staying. Remembering his long-ago first-aid training, Henry reaches for the ice bucket, takes a plastic bag that has contained one of Amy's presents, puts ice in the bag, wraps it in paper napkins and places the wrapped ice pack onto Kaylee's swollen ankle. She grimaces through moist eyes.

'Look at that lot, they can't dance, no rhythm,' Debbie bursts out of her shyness, to no one in particular as groups shuffle around the dance floor out of step with the band.

'Okay, Miss Strictly, we all know you can do a Charleston.' Amy wants to be the centre of attention, but with Kaylee's sprained ankle and Debbie vying for the limelight, it's a losing battle.

'Debbs is like that girl on "Strictly", she's proper good.' Kaylee winces as she moves her leg.

'I like to dance the Charleston,' says Henry smiling at the shy girl as she sinks back into her shell.

'Go on, Debbs; show Grandad what you can do.'

Henry stands up, slips off his jacket to hang on the back of his chair and goes to take Debbie's hand. She hangs back for a moment before she lets Henry escort her to the floor.

'Not the best music, but let's have a go.' Henry smiles at the girl, a good six inches taller than he stands. 'Can you dance in those heels? We don't want another sprained ankle.'

Debbie slips off her shoes and slides them across the floor to the table. Henry flexes his knees and taps a rhythm with his foot. Uncertain, at first, Debbie takes up the beat and they are away. Other couples, girls with boys, girls together, ease back until a wide circle forms around the two dancers. The band, seeing their step, pick up the rhythm as Henry increases the beat and he and his young partner flick their legs and swing their arms to the tempo of 1920s America.

Henry feels as if he were forty years younger and back at the Blackpool Tower Ballroom, the years in-between slipping away. Debbie follows his lead, the floor clears, the band plays with them and everyone claps out the beat.

After hectic minutes, challenged by his rush of energy, and needing to rest, Henry escorts Debbie back to their table as Amy and her friends cheer.

Henry looks at Kaylee. Despite the ice pack her swollen ankle is giving her pain.

'Come on young lady, I'm getting you a taxi and we're off to A&E. You need that ankle treated, or it will be worse by morning. You could have torn a ligament.'

A man in a tight suit comes over and introduces himself as the club's manager.

'That's the best dancing we've had here for many a year. This used to be the major dance hall in the district.'

'Was this the Wyndam Hall?' asks Henry, pausing from his glass of water. 'They held the county finals here in my youth. Young Debbie is the one to congratulate, it was her idea. Now I have to get this young lady to A&E.'

Fifteen minutes later with a blue light flashing, a paramedic is easing Kaylee's pain, as she and Henry are sped through the evening traffic to the hospital.

Mrs Patel, in early morning summer light, stands on the steps to the front door of Unicorn Apartments, watching in amazement as a huge pink car threads its way through the gates and comes slowly up the drive.

Eight young ladies climb out, the last of them struggling with a pair of crutches, her ankle bound tight with a bandage. Then all, but the last of them, hold their wine glasses in the air, four on each side, as they help Henry, still clasping his rolled-up umbrella, out of the limousine, cheering and toasting him for the exciting party they have had.

As Henry walks to the steps, each girl in turn kisses his cheek.

Kaylee grasps his hand. 'When my ankle is better, you will teach me to Charleston, Henry. Promise, you will.'

'I promise, I will.'

Henry turns to his landlady, silent at the top of the steps. 'Good evening, or should it be good morning, Mrs Patel? I have been to a party.'

THE TIPPING PUTT

The November dawn broke at twenty minutes after seven, shedding its weak light on frosted meadows, illuminating scores of spider webs woven across faded summer thistles.

Percy finished the morning milking; five beasts through the parlour, two others in the linhay waiting on winter calves. Percy had one churn of milk to roll out to the stand for the village dairyman, the other, the smaller churn, he took to the farmhouse to make butter and cream.

This was a big day for the farm. Word had come through the cart was ready, the tipping putt his father, Edmund Adams, had discussed at Bridgwater market with Walter Winslade. Percy was to take Betsy, their working horse, walking her eight miles over to collect the cart. Walter, the Shearston blacksmith, had made the metal fittings at his forge, his friend, Jim Porter, the Thurloxton wheelwright, had built the cart.

It was quiet in the lanes, but on the thoroughfare there were motor vehicles; they didn't pause when passing. Percy kept chatting to the horse, near twenty years old and three years his senior, keeping her calm.

Father had said Percy wasn't to go to France; he was needed on the farm, but he would be conscripted once he had his eighteenth birthday. True he was doing much of the farm work, and had been since he was thirteen, leaving school when his brother, Giles, volunteered. Percy had made his mind up to go if the war wasn't ended; Father would get by somehow. They all missed Giles.

Once on the lane up to Shearston, away from the motor lorries, Betsy had a lighter step. The vehicle noises had unnerved her.

'Mr Winslade, I'm Edmund's boy, come to collect the cart.'

'It isn't here, boy; you'll need to get to Jim Porter's yard. It's there and ready, bright as a button in its paintwork.'

'Where do I find he?'

'I'll get the maid to guide you,' and he shouted to the house. 'Phoebe.'

Percy watched the girl, judging her a year or two younger than himself. She dried her hands on her apron, looked to her father then at Percy, sizing him up.

'You take young Percy to Jim Porter's yard.'

They walked the mile to Thurloxton, striding either side of the horse. 'You want to get up on Betsy, Phoebe?'

'You think I can't walk.'

They walked on, not talking, turning in by the wheelwright's cottage. In front of the workshop stood the cart, its reds and blues brilliant in the mid-morning sunshine.

Hesitant at first, then in a full peal, the church bells rang out. Percy watched Jim Porter standing proud by the tipping putt, the long shafts resting on a trestle ready for the horse.

'Why're the bells ringing, Mr Porter? 'Tis Monday today.'

'Don't you know, Phoebe; it's the Armistice, the war is finished.'

'And the lads will be home for Christmas?' Phoebe clutched Jim Porter's hand.

Jim looked over to Percy. 'Not all of them back home, Phoebe.'

The young man fiddled with the buckles on Betsy's traces. Phoebe turned, her blonde locks ruffling in the breeze, she reached up and kissed Percy's cheek.

SUMMER PICTURES

The boys seldom get out of bed until it's too late for breakfast.

'Stay cool Mother, we'll get something at break.'

Maybe they will, probably they won't. Does it matter? Now fifteen and sixteen they've grown taller than their father. Wendy sat with a cup of coffee waiting for the post. Day after day the same scenario was repeated; Tony up and out of the house to his tedious job saying nothing and the boys rushing for school leaving chaos in their wake.

The postman brought three bills, several items of junk mail and an unpleasant bank statement. There were compensations; the day was hot, Tony and the boys were stuck indoors all day; she was enjoying the sun.

She parked at the supermarket glad she was dressed for summer finding the frock from their Greek holiday two summers back. It was revealing, but she knew she looked good. What was the point in making interesting meals when the family never sat down together; half an hour before a meal was ready one of the boys would make himself a wedge of a cheese sandwich, or Tony would go out to the pub promising to be back in time, which he seldom was.

Wendy picked up tins of beans, sliced loaves and a large jar of peanut butter. That was Tony and the boys seen to, she muttered to herself and decided to shop for her own meal.

The shelves displayed ideas for summer salads, leaves she knew and things she'd never seen. She leaned across a cabinet to reach an unfamiliar pack and caught the eye of an elderly man staring down her cleavage. Annoyed, as much with herself as with him, she gave him a withering look.

In the next aisle the same man stood with his hand basket, dithering, blocking the way. Without thinking she pushed her trolley onto the back of his legs, he turned around, a kind and gentle old man. Wendy mumbled an apology and went to the far end of the store to check out, flushed with embarrassment.

She sat in her car, the seats almost too hot for comfort, opening the windows to let the breeze blow through. The old man came out of the store limping and using a trolley for support.

He paused, hearing footsteps, turning as she reached him. He raised his hand to his panama hat.

'I must apologise. I was careless with my trolley. I see you're hurt.'

'It is nothing.' He looked at her. 'It is I who should apologise to you, Madam, for my lapse of manners.'

Wendy blushed at being found out. 'Let me help you with your trolley, at least I can do that for you. Is your car here?

'I live just around the corner. I'll put my shopping into this bag and leave the trolley here.'

There were only a few things in the bottom of the trolley. She remembered he was using a hand basket when she first saw him. Wendy noticed a bloodstain on the back of his light twill trousers.

'I think your leg is bleeding. Let me walk back with you.' Wendy didn't wait for his answer; she scooped up his purchases, putting them into his soft leather bag. Leaving the trolley behind she offered him her arm.

'This is most kind of you. It's not far. I try to get in early to the store, but I never get so charming a companion to assist me home.'

'It's the least I can do.' Wendy glanced at the old man, she guessed in his eighties, much the age her father would have been. Judging by his few purchases he lived on his own. He held her arm in a tight grip as they walked along the street.

Howard Matthews was a man of habit, rising early every day, tidying his flat, shaving, having a shower and getting dressed before sitting down to toast and a cup of coffee. Over breakfast he would decide what he needed for his main meal, a single meal in mid-afternoon.

Wendy went into his flat with him, insisting he sit down to take the weight off his leg. She was concerned at the support he'd taken holding her arm as they walked back to his flat.

'Now, Mr Matthews, you must let me look at your leg. It is Mr Matthews isn't it?'

'How do you know?'

'I looked at the bell pushes by the front door. I hope you don't mind.'

'That was quick of you, but now you have the advantage of me,'

'I'm Wendy, Wendy Parton. Shall I make us both a cup of coffee? Then I can take a look at your injured leg. Just point me to the kitchen.'

'My leg is fine.'

When she returned he was inspecting his leg, his sock rolled down and trouser riding up to show an unfurling bandage. He looked up, hoping she hadn't noticed.

'Don't worry; I'm rather good with bandages. My boys are always getting into scrapes and needing attention.' His bandage was damp from bleeding and seepage from an ulcerating wound on the back of his leg. 'Was this dressing done for you at the surgery?'

'Yes, I caught my leg on the corner of that low table a couple of weeks ago; it's slow to heal. I go to see the nurse on Mondays and Fridays for her to check the dressing, but it came undone last night and I tried to do it up. I don't think I did it too well.'

'Not too bad, but I can do it better for you. Have you been given spare bandages?'

'I have them in the bathroom.'

Once the bandage was fixed Wendy relaxed over coffee, enjoying her new friendship with Mr Matthews in his uncluttered flat. He'd worked as a civil servant in London until he and his wife had moved to Somerset. His wife died not long afterwards.

'This is my son and his family.' He lifted a photograph in a wooden frame from a coffee table to show her. 'I see them every two years when they come home on leave. They can't stay here, it is far too small; they always came to stay when we had the house and their children were small.'

'These are your grandchildren?'

'They are much older now.'

'You have many pictures on your walls. Do you collect them?'

'I suppose I do.'

'Did you paint any of them?' Wendy saw there were several by the same hand, small and subtle watercolours.

'Yes, a number are mine, and a couple were done by Judith, my wife.'

Walking back to her car she regretted her mean purchases earlier and went back to the supermarket to buy something special to cook for the family.

Howard Matthews wandered around his flat looking at the paintings on the walls; they were all done years ago. He resolved to get out his painting things after he'd eaten his afternoon meal and had his sleep, but the box was stowed away in the attic.

The shower was hot on her already tingling skin as she soaped herself washing off the sweat and dirt from the afternoon's gardening. She felt good, pleased with her day, standing with the cascade of water flowing down her body. As she dried she watched herself in the full-length mirror, throwing aside the towel. She held up her shoulder-length hair over her head and looked at the line of her body. Not bad for mid-forties; there wasn't the vibrancy and silkiness of the young girl who'd lain naked on sun-soaked beaches in south-west France, but it wasn't bad for a middle-aged mother of two teenage boys. She dressed to go downstairs and start cooking the supper.

A door slammed as the boys arrived back from school. There was a shout from the hall but neither came in to see what she was doing in the kitchen, despite the enticing smell wafting into the hallway. There was a loud thumping upstairs as two competing sound systems broke into life. For a while the house reverberated with the latest hits.

'Hi Mum!'

'Hello stranger, where's your brother.'

'He's in a mood and sulking. Smells good, are you having people in or something? I've got to go Mum.'

'I've made us all supper. You can't go out, Paul.'

'Got to, Mum. It's cricket nets.'

'It's not Wednesday.'

'This is extra, I've got to go every evening and I might get picked for Saturday.'

'But you'll miss the supper I've cooked for us all.' Wendy looked at her son remembering herself at his age. 'I guess you'll have to go to your cricket. Get picked or I won't forgive you.'

'Thanks Mum.' He added, grabbing a pork pie from the fridge, 'Do you know Dad's gone to Birmingham?'

'He never said.'

'He left a message on the answerphone.'

'What did he say, is he away tonight?

'Back tomorrow, must rush, see you, Mum.' And he was gone, jumping on his bike in the yard and pedalling off towards school.

Wendy took a glass from the sideboard, poured wine from the bottle she'd opened to cook the casserole and went out onto the terrace to enjoy the last of the sun.

'What's for supper, Mum?' A voice called from the bathroom window.

'Baked beans and a fried egg, do you?'

'Great! I thought it might be some fancy stuff from the smell.'

She didn't use the lift at the flats, choosing the stairs despite the burden of her basket bearing last night's supper. Howard Matthews must have seen her car arrive; he was waiting on the landing.

'This is a treat.' He hovered beside her as she came into the flat. 'Is there anything else for me to fetch? I've put new potatoes on to boil as you asked.'

'Wonderful, do you like spinach? It's freshly picked from the garden this morning.'

'A favourite, I grew rows of it when I had a garden.'

Wendy unpacked her square basket. He'd turned on his oven as she'd asked; she put the heavy casserole dish in to heat through. On the balcony off his sitting room he'd set out a bottle of sherry and two glasses. She was glad she'd made the effort to dress up for their lunch date, wearing a blue flower patterned summer dress and heels. Matthews wore a linen jacket with a rose in the button hole.

Wendy told him of her effort to cook a family meal. From time to time, she went through to the kitchen to check how the meal was coming along. He opened the hatch doors in the kitchen to show her the dining room where he'd laid places and put two vegetable dishes to heat on the electric hot plate. There was a bottle of wine on the sideboard standing in a cooler.

'It is kind of you to bring this excellent meal over.'

'You haven't tried it yet.'

'The smell of it wafting from the kitchen is enough to foretell how good it will be.'

'I've had a glass of sherry and I haven't even asked you about the dressing on your leg.'

'It is comfortable and has stayed just as you did it, far better than at the surgery.'

The chicken casserole proved every bit as good as Wendy had hoped. They talked of all manner of things as they ate. She'd brought no pudding, but Howard produced Stilton and water biscuits. After searching in a corner cupboard in the dining room he brought a decanter of port to the table to round off their meal. It was well into the afternoon; he refused to let her wash the dishes, he'd do it later.

But he asked her to help him get his box of painting equipment down from the attic. He'd mentioned it on the phone when she'd rung to invite herself for lunch. As a precaution she'd put a T-shirt, trainers and a pair of jeans into the basket, expecting the attic would be dusty.

'This is the joy of being a top-floor flat. I get the attic for storage.'

'Is there much up there?'

'It's really odds and ends, but there is the box with my drawing things. I didn't mean it to go up there, but my helpers worked too fast.'

Wendy put on her T-shirt and jeans; it was hot in the attic from the sunshine on the roof tiles, in moments she was sweating as she looked over the stack of boxes next to surplus dining room chairs, a large but damaged light shade and suitcases. Bed sheets were draped loosely over the pile. Howard climbed up the first few steps of the ladder to see into the attic.

'Mr Matthews, you must be careful.'

'I'm safe just here. I can point out the box; it says something about apples on it.'

Wendy pulled the sheets back. 'There are labels.'

'Yes, it is labelled; "Drawing books, paints and brushes", or something like that, I think.'

‘Photographs, maps, income tax,’ Wendy called out as she looked at the labels, squinting in the modest light from the single bare bulb.

‘Any luck?’

‘Not yet. Ah! This may be it, it has “Apples” written on it, and, yes, this says “Drawing and Painting”.’

With difficulty, she manoeuvred the old apple box to the edge of the hatch. Howard showed her how to tie a piece of webbing, kept in the attic, around the box to let it slide down the ladder. He reached up from the landing and eased the box’s descent to the floor. Like a boy with a Christmas present he pulled the box along the landing to the sitting room using the webbing strap. Hot and dusty from her exertion, Wendy watched Howard empty the apple box, handling everything as an old friend, putting them out on the table. There were several black tinplate water paint sets, such as she remembered having as a child, a bundle of painting brushes of assorted sizes, rolls of masking tape and a number of sketch books.

He was reluctant to let her look through the sketch books saying they were just notebooks with much unfinished. There were dates on each of the front covers, sometimes a single year, more often spanning two or three years.

‘The books were my wife’s idea. Judith said I ought to keep the drawings I did on odd bits of paper. She gave me that first book in the summer before we were married.’ The cover was marked “1938,” and in another hand “to 1941”.

‘You were married in 1939?’

Wendy smiled, he nodded, she leafed through the earliest book, mostly pencil drawings, some small paintings and a number of pen and ink drawings of buildings. Some drawings were dated, some were finished, but others looked as if just a few thoughts had been sketched down to return to later. Amongst the buildings and landscape sketches were drawings of people, usually a face, sometimes a head and shoulders, most in uniform.

'Are these people you soldiered with during the war?'

'Most of them are, let me see if I recognise anyone. It was a long time ago. I can remember a few names. Some may even still be alive. I was younger than most of them. I know a few didn't see the end of the war.'

'I didn't mean to pry into your past.'

In a later volume covering the late 1940s and early 50s Wendy came across delicate sketches of a naked woman, in some she was pregnant and then later ones with an infant at her breast, intimate pictures, finely drawn in pencil.

'That's Judith and Tim, such a happy time and some of my best drawings.'

'These are exquisite. Do you mind me looking at them?

'I'm flattered you want to see them. I didn't draw them to hide them away, but apart from Judith few people have seen them.'

'They ought to be framed and on your wall. They are some of the most sensitive drawings I've seen; I love them.'

Wendy returned to the drawings of Howard's wife and child after she'd thumbed through later books.

'There's a shower in the spare room if you want to use it when you change.'

'I must. I couldn't put my dress on like this, or drive home in these scruffy things.'

Howard got out a large bath towel and a wrapped bar of soap from an airing cupboard. The flow of water over her body cleansed and calmed her from the excitement of Howard's intimate pictures. She wished she and Tony had such mementos of their adventure bringing their two boys into their family. She wrapped herself in the huge bath towel and gazed at the steamed mirror. Her sweat-soaked underclothes were too horrible to put on. She put on her dress and rolled up the rest in her jeans and pushed them into the basket alongside the casserole dish Howard had washed.

It was hard to sleep that night; no breeze stirred the summer air in their bedroom as Tony lay snoring beside her. Wendy tossed the duvet off her side of the bed.

She decided to take Howard for a picnic in the country. He'd told her how much he'd enjoyed expeditions to favoured haunts with his sketchbook before he gave up driving.

She was jealous of Judith, his wife. Poor soul, she'd been dead for a dozen years, almost since the younger of her two sons was at playschool, yet she thought of the drawing of her lying on her bed before her child was born, and later sitting in a low chair with the infant boy at her breast; she envied her such wonderful drawings.

'This is kind of you Wendy. I feel guilty monopolising so much of your time.'

'Don't worry on that score. Tony is at work, the boys at school and the house is as neat as it will ever be. I was up with the birds this morning getting everything done so we could have a good day out.'

'Thank you, and for all the good works you have done on my leg. It is healing well. You are a wonderful nurse. I don't need to go to the surgery tomorrow.'

'You should look in to have it seen, even if they sign you off.'

'We must turn left at this next junction, where that red car is coming out.'

'I don't think I've ever been into the country out this way, into these hills.'

'And it's the right day for it, blue sky and long views.'

Howard had been waiting outside the flats, his basket packed with a flask of hot water to make tea or coffee, a bottle of wine and a fruit cake he'd bought that morning from the WI shop. It made a good picnic with the sandwiches Wendy brought. Two sketch books, a box of paints and small screw top jars, once used for mustard, now holding water for his painting, filled out his basket.

Once off the main road the lane climbed further as grasses and bracken, flowers and occasional brambles brushed the sides of the car before they came to a wide rough mown verge under an old beech tree casting a welcome shade.

'Here we are. It hasn't changed much over the years.' Howard pointed to a gap in the hedge bank with a stile, the way marked with a wooden sign showing a public footpath.

Wendy made two journeys between the car and their chosen picnic spot looking out across the valley. She worried Howard might damage his leg again, determined to carry something of their picnic burden. He took it slowly, managing to climb the stile without mishap.

As soon as they were settled he opened his sketch book and started to draw, looking at the view across the vale, over the town almost flickering in the day's heat and to the hills a dozen miles away. Wendy spread out the picnic on the rug between them. He worked his pencil at speed with few lines on the paper before the shapes in the landscape became recognisable. For an hour he worked on a series of drawings, moving easily from one to the other, adding depth with shading, going on to start another before going back to add to an earlier drawing. He paused from time to time to eat a sandwich or to take a drink of wine; Wendy rationed herself to a single glass. Little was said between them, Howard was absorbed into his task, Wendy relaxed lying back in the grass, her eyes closed in the sunlight.

'I am so enjoying this.' He smiled at her as he spoke. 'You have broken my routine, doing the same thing at the same time of day. I am grateful to you. I don't know how I can repay you.'

'You don't have to. I'm getting as much enjoyment as you are and this place is idyllic. It must be beautiful all year round, not just in summer; imagine the autumn with the trees turning to their flaming colours.'

'I used to come here a lot. I once did a large painting of it in autumn time. I put it into an exhibition and it was sold on the first day. I was very pleased.'

'I wish I'd bought it.'

'That's what I will do, then. I will paint you a picture.'

'I would love that,' Wendy laughed, 'I don't want to go home, I want this day to last forever and ever. Is that daft?'

'Not at all, there are some days like that, but we'll have to go home sometime.'

'Howard.' Wendy sat up, 'Howard would you mind if I sunbath here while you are drawing?'

'Not at all, you enjoy yourself. I don't want you getting bored.'

'But I mean taking my top off to sunbathe properly.' The beauty of their picnic place, the heat of the day, and no doubt the wine with the picnic, all combined to make her want to be free from her sweatshirt and jeans.

'Whatever you want, Wendy, I'll get on with my drawing.'

She peeled off her things to lie back in the summer grass, feeling the sun caressing her whole body.

Three weeks later, Howard rang to ask her to come round for lunch. They'd met once since their glorious summer picnic, Wendy asking if he'd completed her picture. He laughed and told her it would take longer as he had to work on it, building it up from his sketches and he wanted it to be just right for her.

Now it was promised. She was excited as she climbed the stairs to his flat. An easel stood in the corner of his sitting room on which rested a picture covered under a piece of cloth. Howard asked her to stand on the far side of the room before he lifted the cover.

The picture, mounted in a beechwood frame, was everything she wanted, its subtle watercolour in his style she so liked in the pictures she'd seen on his walls. She rushed over to look at it closer while he stood aside beaming. Wendy threw her arms around his shoulders and kissed his cheek.

When she left the flat he handed her a second package, about half the size of the picture, carefully wrapped in brown paper telling her she could only open it when she got home, and was on her own.

Once home she placed the landscape painting on the dining room table, then sat on the sofa to unwrap her mystery present, thinking it might be one of the paintings she had admired hung on his walls.

She looked at it in wonder, a tingle zipping up her spine. She'd no idea he'd drawn her as she lay sunbathing naked on their picnic, recognisable and drawn as beautifully as the sketches of his wife and son in his early sketchbook. It was the best present he could have given her.

She hung both pictures, the landscape in the sitting room, taking down a print they'd kept on their walls since they were married, and the sketch of her lying in the grass on their bedroom wall. For several days Tony failed to notice.

She was in the bath after an afternoon's gardening before they were due to go out to a party when a shout came from the bedroom.

'Good grief, this is a picture of you. Where on earth did this come from?'

She never did tell him where it came from, but they never got to their party either.

THE RELUCTANT SAMARITAN

It was not good enough. Percy Travers sat in his chair - Lottie and he had reached the stage in life when they had their own sitting room chairs - and stared at the television screen, at the rain falling at Lords. It was a fine day in Percy's corner of Somerset, but at Lords there was rain and the commentators thought it unlikely there would be any play on the opening day of the First Test.

Percy had set aside the day to watch cricket on the box, not least as he had a modest wager on the number of runs and wickets there would be on the scoreboard before lunch, and then by teatime, on the first day. Although it was fine in the garden he was not going to start work outside. With a twinge of conscience, he ignored the imagined voice of his absent wife reminding him of his outside jobs; the vegetable bed needed hoeing and the lawn in want of mowing.

Her absence was part of the problem. Yet again her older sister was supposedly ill and Lottie insisted her place was by her sister's side which meant his long planned three-day excursion to Founder's Day at his old university wasn't happening for him. He had to stay at home to look after the dog and to tend to the recent acquisition of five rescued battery hens in their enclosure at the bottom of the garden, another of Lottie's enthusiasms.

Fifty years ago, as a precocious scholarship boy, he had gone up to university to emerge three years later with the modest award of a 2:2. He had never returned over the years, but months ago he'd decided it was time he went back. He would no longer feel bested by his contemporaries, some of whom he had read of in newspapers receiving honours, and even two he knew of with peerages. Retired from his humdrum career he could exaggerate its merit, if challenged. It no longer mattered to him, although he couldn't say the same of Lottie. When a workmate and his wife had gone to London to represent the company at a Buckingham Palace Garden Party she spoke of it for days in questioning tones. He didn't think it wise to tell her they had drawn lots in the office as to who should go to Buckingham Palace.

So Percy decided to go out for a drive, nowhere in particular, a drive into the countryside away from their village home.

He'd not been motoring for more than twenty minutes when, on a narrow lane, he passed a car awkwardly parked on the verge. He drove by, but, as he turned the bend further along the lane, he caught sight in his driving mirror of a person attempting to make a phone call. Percy smiled, there was no chance of any mobile signal in these parts.

Percy had motored another half mile when he realised what it was he had seen in his driving mirror, and had passed on by. The attempting caller was a woman, she was wearing some sort of uniform and the car was at an angle, probably with a wheel stuck in the ditch.

But it wasn't his business and he drove on.

Yet at the next junction he turned right, then again onto the main road. Someone was bound to have passed the stranded car and its driver, but with one more right turn he was back on the original lane. He could check all was well and get on pursuing his nowhere-in-particular journey.

But all wasn't well; the car appeared to be abandoned until he drew level and a District Nurse stood up from her futile effort to lift the front bumper. Percy paused then got out of his car.

'There's no signal,' she said.

'Not around here. What's the trouble?'

'A delivery van, the wretched driver pushed past and I seem to have got a wheel stuck in the soft verge; I can't get the car out.'

Percy bent down to have a look. 'It might be worse than that, you've hit a large stone.'

'That's all I need, I'm already late. I don't suppose you have a mobile that works. I need to ring base so they can sort something out.'

'I'm afraid I don't, no one does, there's no signal around here.'

'Perhaps together we could lift the car to get it out.'

'I don't think so.'

The nurse looked at him, disbelieving her day was unravelling.

'How about I drive you to your next call. There's a garage run by a man I know about five miles away. He could do something to get the car out. I could get him onto it while you do your calls. Have you got many to do?'

'Half a dozen.'

'I could be your chauffeur for today. I've not got anything special arranged.'

Ten minutes later, with the nurse's bag of medical supplies transferred to Percy's car, they had introduced themselves and arrived at her next patient's bungalow. Yvonne Simpkins, SRN, got out in a hurry, took her case from the back seat and smiled at Percy. 'Are you sure you want to take me on my round this afternoon?'

'It'll be a new experience for me. How long do you think you'll be here?'

'I'll be at least half an hour. Miss Thorne will be anxious I've arrived so late. Do you mind waiting?'

'I'll go to the garage and get them to recover your car. Do you have your ignition key?'

'They should be able to get it going where it is, won't they?'

'It'll be a bit more than stuck in the mud after hitting that rock. I can get to the garage and back before you're done here.'

With that agreed, Nurse Yvonne went in to see Miss Thorne and Percy set off for the garage.

By six o'clock they had covered all of Yvonne's calls for the day and were at the garage. Her mud-splashed car stood abandoned outside the workshop.

'It needs parts. The nearside track rod is damaged.'

'Will that take long?' the District Nurse asked.

'If the parts come in the morning it'll be ready late tomorrow, if they come in the second delivery, it'll be the next morning. Leave your number and we'll ring when we know.'

'I'm working tomorrow, but you can leave a message. I've got a number to ring to get a back-up vehicle for the day.'

As he drove Yvonne to her home Percy's stomach rumbled. 'Have you had lunch?' he asked.

'No, and I've left my sandwiches with the car.'

'I could do with a bite. Do you fancy a pub supper, or is Mr Simpkins waiting for you?'

'It's just me... and my lad.'

'Would he like a pub supper?' Percy asked as he remembered the dog left all day at home and the chickens yet to be fed.

'No, he's off at university. Tell you what, I'll buy us supper to thank you for this afternoon, my treat. But I need to go home and get changed first.'

'I'll drop you home then go back to feed my dog and see the hens are alright, then I'll get back to pick you up at half seven. Would The Lamb and Flag be good for you? They do good fish suppers.'

'Will Mrs Travers be coming?'

'She's away seeing her sister. And you don't need to ring for any back-up tomorrow. I can run you round your patients again.'

'I'll have to buy you a dessert as well then, but thank you; it's helpful having a chat between visits and not having to concentrate on the road all the time.'

They were playing at Lords on the second day, but Percy was happy driving the District Nurse around her patch. He tuned in to Test Match Special while she was with her patients, but turned the radio off as soon as she came back to the car.

'Shall we go to the pub for lunch?'

'Not while I'm on duty. I've made enough sandwiches for both of us. There's a good spot for a quick picnic down by the lake. I often go there when I'm on my rounds.'

Yvonne had been in touch with the garage. They needed more parts than they had at first ordered. They expected the car to be ready for the third day, but that wasn't one of her working days. She smiled, telling Percy he could stand down from his chauffeuring duties.

'I expect my wife will be home tomorrow, even she grows tired of her sister's constant complaints after a few days.'

'Have you ever thought of volunteering to drive for the hospital. They're very short of volunteers, always seeking people to help driving patients in and out when they have no transport.'

'I can't say I've ever thought about it.'

Two days later, Lottie and Percy were in town shopping. They called into their regular stop-off for a cup of coffee and a bun. Lottie chose a table while Percy went to the counter to collect their order. He had to wait as the person queuing in front of him ordered, then changed her mind, for what appeared to be a group of five people. He paid and picked up his tray with their coffee and buns. It was never easy carrying a tray in the crowded space and with the coffee mugs filled to the brim sitting on modernistic lop-sided saucers.

There was another woman seated at Lottie's table with her back to him. As he put down the tray, Lottie said to the woman, 'This is my husband. I don't think you two have met. Percy, this is Yvonne, sorry I can't remember your surname, dear.'

From the look on Percy's face, Yvonne guessed he hadn't spoken to Lottie of their two-day adventure.

'Do you want a coffee, Yvonne? Percy will get it for you. Yvonne comes to the still life painting classes I go to at the Arts Centre.'

'No, I've already had a cup, Lottie. I must be getting on. Pleased to meet you, Mr Travers, I think our paths must have crossed somewhere before now.'

'Yvonne is a District Nurse, Percy.'

'I was thinking of volunteering as a patient transfer driver for the hospital.'

'That is good, Mr Travers, they're always short of volunteers.'

'Whatever has brought that on, Percy? You've never said anything about it before.'

ABOUT THE AUTHOR

After national service in the army, Chip Tolson worked in the coastal and international ship-owning industries in Liverpool, in the Far East and in Edinburgh over thirty-five years. In recent times he and his wife, Clare, have lived in a one-time farmhouse with twelve hilly acres on Exmoor, looking after rough grazing land, tending chickens and planting a woodland.

Amongst the twenty-three short stories published in *PEBBLES*, three have won prizes in the Yeovil Literary Prize International Short Story Competition.

ISLAND SUMMER won second prize in 2012,

LET IT BE ANTHEA won first prize in 2013, and

HENRY'S HEN NIGHT won first prize in 2015.

On the back cover: A Prize decorated pebble on a seaside theme, Camilla Tolson.

OTHER WORK BY CHIP TOLSON

With his short film script, *SANDSCAPE ARTIST*, Chip won Somerset Film's 2014/15 Scriptwriting Competition. Sandscape Artist was filmed on location at Burnham-on-Sea in July 2016 and will be released later in the year.

Chip's fable, *THE BATTLE OF SLOTTERHAM HALL, AD 1929*, in which the Pheasants resolve to confront the Shoot, was published as an e-book on Amazon in 2014.

Chip's novel, *REQUIEM FOR PRIVATE HUGHES*, in which the ambitions of a Somerset lad, Archie Middlebrook, are shattered in a terrorist ambush in Malaya, and Private Hughes is killed, was published as a paperback and e-book on Amazon in 2015. Four decades pass before Archie comes to terms with the trauma in his youth to celebrate the life of his friend and fellow national serviceman, Geraint Hughes.

Chip's next novel, *THE REGISTER OF JOE'S TREES*, will be published in 2017. The novel tells the tale of the decades that follow a teenager's affair with a US airman, whose life is lost on a bombing raid over Europe in 1943.

www.chiptolson.com